Crispin's Castle

PATHFINDER SERIES

1 *Crispin's Castle*, by Kathleen M. Duncan
2 *Sally and the Shepherdess*, by Kathleen M. Duncan
3 *The Gypsy*, by Janet Kippax
4 *The Wreck of the Pied Piper*, by C. N. Moss
5 *The Runaway Girl*, by Beryl J. Read
6 *Armada Quest*, by Irene Way

Crispin's Castle

KATHLEEN M. DUNCAN

OF THE ZONDERVAN CORPORATION
GRAND RAPIDS, MICHIGAN 49506

Published in 1967

Published by Zondervan Publishing House in the USA by special arrangement with Pickering and Inglis Ltd. of London and Glasgow.

Zondervan Edition 1979

Library of Congress Cataloging in Publication Data

Duncan, Kathleen M
Crispin's castle.

(Pathfinder series)
SUMMARY: An orphan with no hint of his identity, Crispin moves in with the Bernard family, where he feels strongly at home in the shadow of an old English castle and discovers his true identity.
[1. Orphans—Fiction. 2. England—Fiction]
I. Title. II. Series.
PZ7.D9116Cr [Fic] 78-21525
ISBN 0-310-37821-4

Printed in the United States of America

CONTENTS

*The characters in this book are entirely imaginary,
and bear no relation to any living person.*

1

Six, and One Extra!

"Give a cheer, somebody!" said Mother, getting stiffly out of the car. "We're here at last!"

"I'm not cheering yet," answered Dad, resting his arms on the steering wheel, "not till we're really inside—we've probably forgotten to bring the key or something!"

Simon unwound himself from the hamper and two suitcases which had boxed him in through the whole long trip. "Don't say that!" he groaned. "I could go to sleep standing up—Jon and Beth are asleep already."

Dad glanced at his two youngest in the dim glow from a streetlight. They were slumped together on the back seat, and Jon was still clutching his ball bat.

Jenny, the older sister, edged away from them, and struggled out to join her mother. "If we leave them there, Dad," she said, "I guess you and Simon could carry them in later, and they'd never wake up till tomorrow."

"You're uncommonly sensible sometimes," her father told her, "though Beth is a weight to carry! Have you the key, Mother? Then you shall unlock the door and take possession on behalf of the Bernard family!"

Mother hesitated, her hand on the garden gate on which the name 'Sunnyhill' showed faintly. "Is it safe to leave the car with them in it?"

"Safe as houses—I've run it against the curb to make certain," Dad told her.

Jenny, suddenly feeling wide awake again, called, "Come on, Mother! I'm dying to get inside—it's the first house we've ever had of our very own!"

The steep little street was silent as they went up the garden path. Few lights were on in the houses on either side. Then, from somewhere far below came the hooting of a tug. Simon said, "Listen! I'd forgotten the harbor would be so close! It's going to be super living here!"

It should have been a very different homecoming, Mother thought. They had planned to arrive in the morning, before the furniture van could get there, and have the whole afternoon to get beds made and put up curtains.

But halfway through the long drive from the Midlands to Dover, the car had broken down. So here they were, at nearly ten o'clock on that warm September night, with a houseful of furniture and packing cases, dumped where the moving men had fancied.

"Well, it's just no good being tired—we've got to get somewhere ready to sleep—that's all that matters tonight." Dad squared his shoulders and tried to forget that he'd been driving all day.

Jenny was already opening doors, switching on lights, and not caring how late they were because this was the most exciting thing that had ever happened to the family.

As Dad and Simon carried suitcases into the hall she

appeared in the kitchen doorway waving a teakettle, which the moving men had thoughtfully left on top of the gas stove. "Cheer up!" she called, her brown eyes dancing. "This is fun! Let's enjoy it while we're all together, before Dad has to go away!"

"Make way!" called Dad from the front door as he came in with the biggest suitcase which he had taken from the car trunk. "Pull the door wider, Simon. I'm going to skin my knuckles!"

"Won't go," announced Simon. "It's got a big wooden thing on the back of the letter-box."

"I'll take that off for a start," said Dad. "See if there's anything in it, Simon. I gave our change of address last week."

Simon felt in the box and pulled out two envelopes. "Two 'Welcome' cards by the look of it," he said as he handed them over. Then he fished out something else, and added, "Here's a telegram! I wonder how long ago it came?"

Mother sat down on the bottom of the stairs and opened the buff envelope. For a moment she stared at it, and then she exclaimed, "Oh, NO! Not tonight!"

"What is it?" asked the other three as though they were one person.

"It's Crispin!" answered Mother a little faintly. "She—she's sending him for us to take care of!"

"Who's Crispin?" asked Jenny.

"Is he a dog?" demanded Simon. "Who's sending him to be taken care of?"

But Mother was looking reproachfully at Dad. "I expect it was your idea in the first place," she said, "and it looks as if we haven't a chance to say 'No'!"

Dad reached for the telegram, equally worried. "Crispin arriving 10:40 P.M. Monday. Sorry. Unavoidable," he read aloud. "It was sent yesterday from London—the Post Office certainly did their job. It wouldn't have been so bad if we'd arrived this morning."

"But who IS Crispin, Dad?" asked Simon, almost bursting with curiosity.

"That's a long story," answered Dad, helping Mother up, and heading towards the kitchen, "too long to tell you standing around with the front door open—let's see what we can find to sit on."

"Crispin's a funny name," said Jenny, "it reminds me of knights in armor."

"Shakespeare!" murmured Simon. "We had something from his *King Henry* before the battle of Agincourt to learn at school—'We happy few . . . we band of brothers . . .' and it finishes 'gentlemen in England now abed will count themselves accursed they were not with us on St. Crispin's day!"

Mother began to unpack the hamper of food they had brought with them, while Dad rested on a kitchen chair.

"Crispin is a boy your Aunt Anthea takes an interest in," he told them. "She found him years ago in a Greek orphanage, and took a liking to him. But you know Aunt Anthea! She's always away giving lecture tours on zoology or whatever it is!"

"So what did she do with him?" asked Jenny, wide-eyed.

"Put him in schools abroad when he grew too old for nurses, poor little fellow," said her mother, shaking a few stray lumps of sugar out of the bottom of the hamper. "But she keeps changing schools from what I hear. Did she say there was anything wrong with this last one when she met you in London, Dad?"

Dad shook his head. "I believe she told me he was in France—or Holland. She complained that the holidays were difficult, so I said maybe we'd have him one Christmas, that was all."

"So she's gone and dumped him on us now—just when we're moving!" said Simon wrathfully.

"And we don't want anyone but just us while we've got Daddy at home!" protested Jenny. "There won't be room, will there, Mother?" she added. "Simon's got to sleep in the attic as it is!"

"Looks as if I'll have to share it pretty quick, too!"

Simon gloomily picked up the telegram, and read it again. "Arriving 10:40—and that's just about now."

As if to echo his words there was the sound of a car stopping outside, a door slammed, and a man's voice said, "There you are, young Sir, that'll be three and sixpence."

"It's the taxi! Oh, why did he have to come TONIGHT!" wailed Jenny, forgetting the teakettle she still held, as she swung around in a sudden passion of rebellion. The lid flew off, and some water shot over her feet, adding to her misery. As she carried it to the sink, her parents hurried into the hall. She could hear them trying to sound welcoming to the most unwelcome guest.

She stood a moment biting back her tears before she could go out and join them. "I'm being horrid," she told herself. "After all, he can't help not having any relatives, and he probably doesn't want to come and live with us any more than we want him to."

"Jenny!" came her mother's voice. "Is that teakettle on? We'd better all have something to eat—here's another hungry one!"

"Coming," called Jenny, struggling with the unfamiliar faucet, and by the time she had put the teakettle on to boil her tears were dry.

Crispin stood in the hall clutching a battered Airways bag, and an equally old suitcase. "He doesn't look so bad," decided Jenny, taking in at one glance the slight, blond boy. He had very blue eyes, looked younger than his ten years, and seemed a little anxious.

"Here's Crispin!" began Dad, somewhat unnecessarily, when a sad little voice from the front door made them all look around.

Jon stood there, still clutching the plaid rug, which draped around him like the blanket of an Indian squaw. "You left me outside!" he said indignantly and then, suddenly aware of a newcomer, he added, "Who are you?"

"I'm Crispin," answered the visitor, "I—I'm sorry. I'm afraid I shouldn't have come."

Before they could stop him Jon said, with an enormous yawn, "Well, if you're staying with us, I just hope you don't want my building blocks to make things with."

"Jon!" exclaimed his mother sharply, "that's rude!" Jon looked suddenly subdued as he trailed after them into the kitchen.

For a minute there was a tense silence. Then Mother put her hands on Crispin's shoulders, and gave him one of her warm, kind smiles.

"You'll have to forgive us," she said. "We're just a bit unprepared. But don't feel you ought not to have come—if you'll just take us as we are, you're as welcome as the flowers in May!"

"'Specially if you can cook sausages!" exclaimed Jon, who was suddenly ravenous, and even Jenny laughed.

"I'd better go and fetch young Beth in," said Dad, looking relieved. Simon began to search for plates and cups in one of the crates. Mother came across the frying pan in a box of towels, and soon the sausages were sizzling away.

Jenny started to set the table. She had found an odd selection of knives and forks, and Crispin stood watching her. Jenny felt she ought to talk to him, but she just didn't know how to begin. Simon seemed to be struck dumb as well.

Then Dad came in once more, with Beth in his arms. In spite of the voices, and the taxi doors banging, she was still fast asleep, her long blonde hair covering her face, and falling over Dad's shoulder in a silky ripple. "Run up and see where they've put the blankets," he told Simon. "I'm going to lay Beth on a bed just as she is—seems she's too tired even to want supper."

Crispin stared after Dad wide-eyed as he started up the stairs. "How ever many of you are there?" he asked anxiously.

"Six counting Mother and Dad." Jenny smiled at him, her brown eyes suddenly friendly. "You'll make seven," she said, and added, "there's a packet of salt in that crate if you look for it—Dad's sure to want some."

After that everybody began to talk and laugh, and

enjoy their first meal at Sunnyhill, although there was no tablecloth, and Jon had to have orangeade out of the milk pitcher because nobody could find a glass.

"Where did you travel from, to get here I mean?" asked Simon, as he went to fry himself an extra sausage.

"Brussels," answered Crispin, pushing his empty plate away with a satisfied sigh. "At least that's where I started from. Aunt Anthea saw me off from London. She was on her way to New York, you see."

"Wizzo! You do get around, don't you!" Jenny looked at him with growing respect.

Dad asked quietly, "If it's not an awkward question, old boy, just why did your Aunt Anthea want you to come to us?"

"Sorry—I forgot you didn't know," said Crispin. "It was the drains at school, you see. They went wrong or something, and people started getting sick. That is, the people who have to stay at school all the holidays. It's a school down near the French border, and it's awfully old. Suddenly it was closed down—I'd been in Brussels with Aunt Anthea and they just called up and said I couldn't come back."

"So that's how it was!" exclaimed Mother. "Well, it's a good thing that we were here for you to come to. I expect we'll get a letter from New York before long."

She broke off and looked across at Jenny, who was beginning to carry the empty cups to the sink. "I think it had better be bed for you, young lady," she said. "You've gone awfully white, and you must be dead tired. I'll do the dishes, if you help Jon get ready for bed."

"Mommy says the men put all three beds in one

room, so we can have a pillow fight in the morning," announced Jon as he stumped upstairs.

"Hush!" hissed Jenny. "You'll wake Beth!" But she need not have worried. Beth lay with her arms stretched out in the moonlight—no one had unpacked any curtains.

Jon was asleep almost before Jenny could peel his things off, and hustle on his pajamas. She pulled the blankets over him, and ran lightly down to find her mother.

"I was afraid I'd be asleep before you came to kiss us good night," she said, as Mother stopped wiping up to give her a hug.

"Good night, pet, don't forget your prayers. We've got a lot to be thankful for. We did arrive safely after all, and I'm sure we're going to be happy here."

Jenny leaned her cheek for a moment against her mother's warm shoulder.

"I'm glad God made six of us in this family," she said, and they both thought of Crispin, who was one alone.

Crispin at that moment was helping Dad unstrap a roll of sleeping bags, relics of the Bernards' last camping holiday.

"One for you and one for Simon in the attic tonight," said Dad. "We'll fix you up with a camp bed tomorrow, Crispin."

So they clattered up the uncarpeted stairs. Simon, his arms full, butted open the door of the little attic room right up under the roof.

"Guess there's a really great view from here in daylight!" he said.

Crispin gave a cry of delight.

"Look! Look now!" He explained, "We couldn't see it from downstairs—it's fabulous—see the Castle on the hill!"

2
A Door to Adventure

Long after Simon was asleep that night, Crispin wriggled out of his sleeping bag on the attic floor to take one more look at the castle.

It rose above the dark roofs of the town, shining and beautiful in the moonlight. Simon had told him that the greenish glow, which made every archway and turret show clear and strong against the night sky, must be floodlighting. Crispin had never seen anything as old as Dover Castle which looked so perfect. Now that the house was quiet, and even Mr. and Mrs. Bernard had gone to bed, he felt that in some way the castle belonged to him alone.

Leaning his elbows on the windowsill he looked out, feeling as though he was in an ancient turret himself because he was so high above the garden, and Sunnyhill was the highest house of all.

"It's odd," thought Crispin, "but I've got a feeling of belonging here more than in any of the other places I've been—"

Not for the first time he wished fiercely that he knew which country he belonged to. "I'm not Greek, I'm certain," he thought, "not with my hair and eyes. If I knew for sure that I was English, then I'd be proud of that castle. I'd pretend I was one of the Knights who used to live up there—I'd pretend the King had said to me, 'Rise up, Sir Crispin Cotterell!' "

The night wind stirred his hair, and suddenly he shivered. Two minutes later he was curled up in his warm sleeping bag, and with a jumble of castle walls and knights on chargers in his mind, he fell asleep.

Sounds of laughter and the shower running woke him in the morning. Simon's sleeping bag was already empty, and from the noise on the landing it appeared that Beth and Jon were having an argument.

"I tell you he's real!" came Jon's indignant voice. "If you don't believe me, go up and look! You shouldn't sleep so much if you don't want to miss things."

Beth went clattering down into the hall, and Crispin heard her saying, "Mommy—do tell Jon not to be silly—he keeps saying there's a strange boy in the attic!"

Crispin chuckled and yawned, as the voices were lost when the kitchen door slammed. Then he remembered the castle and scrambled up to look at it while he hastily pulled on his clothes. In daylight it looked much bigger. Tinted pink in the early morning sunlight, it seemed to be floating on a bank of sea mist.

Breakfast was fun, and everyone was friendly, except Beth, who gazed at him while she ate her cornflakes, looking slightly resentful.

Crispin couldn't decide whether she was shy, or whether she disliked him because Simon was teasing her about 'the strange boy in the attic.'

At eight years old, Beth hated to be left out of anything that the older members of the family were doing. She wished that five-year-old Jon had been the one carried from the car sound asleep. "It's not fair!" she muttered to herself. "They ought to have told me!"

"What's not fair?" asked Mother promptly. "Don't be in a grizzling mood today, Beth. It's going to be wonderfully hot, and we've all got to work like beavers."

"I get to clean the windows," said Jenny as she buttered Jon's bread for him. "I love really filthy windows—it's so satisfying seeing the dirt running down. There you are, Pieface. I'll do another piece if you want it."

"I get to make a bonfire with all the papers and scraps! Can I, Daddy—can I light the match?" pleaded Jon.

His father answered tactfully, "You can if Crispin will keep an eye on you—we shall be knee deep in paper and shavings by the time all these cases are unpacked."

Simon, it appeared, was going to help Dad move beds and push dressers around, so Crispin found himself Bonfire-maker-in-chief, which was very much to his liking. It was no good, he reflected, trying to go and see the castle that day, much as he wanted to. Everyone was too busy to want to go with him. Anyway, he had never had the fun of moving before. Aunt Anthea always lived in expensive furnished apartments, and moving with the Bernard family seemed to be very entertaining indeed.

It was just the right morning for their first day in a new home. The windows were open wide, and the sun shone in as they worked. The children could hear the sound of Mother singing as she put up the curtains, and the tangled little garden on the top of the hill seemed a wonderful place to have for their own.

"No one's lived here for ages," said Jon, tramping around in the high grass. Beth stood watching butterflies fanning their wings on some early asters by the old wall.

At the end of the garden was a dilapidated woodshed, where Crispin rummaged for some old bricks to make what he called a 'fireplace.'

"Come and help me make a circle of them," he said, enjoying being the 'boss.' "We'll pile all the litter in the middle, and if any pieces fall outside when they're lit, we'll stamp them out."

For a while they went back and forth from the house, dragging out everything that Dad and Simon said could be burned. Then Jon lost interest, and looked for a place where he could climb on the wall, to look out over the other gardens which sloped down the hill.

"Hi!" he called to Crispin and Beth, who were still busy. "Come and look—I can see the harbor!"

They raced to join him, and Crispin helped Beth up till she could rest painfully on her elbows and gaze at the view. She stayed there for two exciting seconds, and then fell with a yelp into a clump of nettles.

It was only a little bit of blue water that they could see, with great cliffs rising above it, and the buildings of the town clustering in the valley below them. But the sea wall, and a lighthouse, showed quite plainly. Jon shouted, "There's a ship! It's coming in—I'm the first one to see a ship! Even Simon hasn't!"

"Simon and Crispin saw the castle last night." Beth

picked herself up and felt her stings gingerly. She always liked taking people down a peg or two, Crispin noticed.

As it happened, it was her turn to find something new a few minutes later. Tracing the line of an overgrown pathway she found to her surprise that it led right around behind the woodshed. Nettles barred her way, but Beth found a big stick with which to beat them down, and there, hidden behind the shed, was a shabby little door in the high wall.

The next minute the boys had joined her. Jenny, coming into the garden with a jug of lemonade and some cake for 'elevenses,' heard excited voices and went to investigate.

"A door!" she said. "Why, I don't believe even Dad knows there's a way out of the garden. See if it opens, Beth—here—let me try."

The jug of lemonade stood forgotten on the path while they wrestled with the stubborn old catch. Even when it loosened they had to jab weeds away from the bottom before the hinges began to creak.

"Wait!" exclaimed Jenny suddenly. "I heard something crying—"

Crispin stopped pulling at the door, and they listened for a second. Then the cry came again, a tiny meow.

"It's in the tangle behind the shed—it's a kitten meowing," said Jenny. In a moment Jon was down on hands and knees, peering under the rotting boards and old oil cans which had been thrown away there.

"Kitty—kitty—" he called hopefully, and with a tiny rustling and another meow, a very small striped kitten came out to greet them.

Beth sat down and coaxed it into her lap.

"Can we keep it?" asked Jon promptly.

But Crispin was certain it had come over the wall. "It isn't too small to climb," he said. "Let's open the door and see where it came from."

A few more tugs, and they were looking out of their own garden into a narrow lane. High walls closed it in on either side, and it was too rough for cars.

"It's odd!" said Beth, "but it's a yummy place to play in!"

"Let's go as far as the bend," suggested Crispin. "I believe it must go downhill pretty steeply—guess it finishes up somewhere in the town."

He ran on and the others trotted after, the kitten clinging with its tiny claws to Beth's thin yellow shirt. A few yards further on they found that the lane widened out, and there were several old garden doors in the walls, like their own.

"I'm going back," said Jenny. "Mother might be worried if none of us is around, and I guess the wasps are getting in the lemonade."

"Was there a piece of Swiss Roll?" asked Jon anxiously. "Ants like that, and they'll make it all mucky."

The thought of food made them race back to the garden. In spite of Jenny's protests, Beth carried the kitten boldly into the kitchen.

Mother was perched on the edge of the table drinking coffee. "Oh, darling, where did you get it?" she cried, "You can't just bring kittens home like that. It must belong to somebody."

"That's what Cris said, but it was in our garden—" began Beth, looking stubborn.

Crispin, who was right behind her, said quickly, "Call me Crispin please. I don't like it shortened."

Beth swung around and stared at him, her blue eyes looking scornful. "Why not?" she demanded. "I'm Elizabeth, but Beth is good enough for me. Jon's Jonathan, but nobody calls him that. Why are you so special if you don't even belong anywhere particular? I know, because Daddy told us."

"Beth!" Mother put down her cup, looking stern indeed, but Beth was near the door. She slipped through, with the kitten clawing its way to the back of her neck as she went. They saw her running towards the woodshed.

Before Mother or Jenny could stop him, Crispin turned and went upstairs, his face set, and very white.

"Oh dear! I wish Beth wasn't so horrible sometimes!" Jenny looked really distressed as they heard him tramping up the wooden steps.

"I'll have a talk with her tonight that she won't like very much," said her mother. "I don't mind teasing. But Beth says things intended to hurt, and it's time she stopped it."

They had forgotten Jon, who was by the window, eating his Swiss Roll in very small pieces to make it last longer. "Granny says voices ought to be used for what God meant them to say," he observed. "I wish Granny had moved with us—"

Mother's expression softened as she looked at him, with his grubby knees and sticky hands. "Good old Jon! I wish Granny was here, too," she said. "She did help you remember God in the small things of everyday, and the small things are the hinges that turn the big ones.

Help Beth to remember that if you can, son. You're not too young to do a job for God."

And then, turning to Jenny, she said briskly, "Go and tell Beth to take that kitten and put it over the wall. Then I expect it will run home. If it keeps coming back we shall have to make inquiries."

Jenny went out slowly, knowing there would probably be a fuss. Jon, throwing the last of his crumbs to an inquisitive sparrow, trailed after her.

3

Behind the Blackberries

Silence descended on the kitchen, except for the sounds of hammering from upstairs, where Dad and Simon were still busy.

Mother went back to her work with a troubled expression. Beth was really getting very tiresome, and it seemed as if Crispin's arrival was going to make matters worse. Jenny had better go up and make peace with him when she came in, because Jenny was a good soother of ruffled feelings.

But she didn't have much time to worry about it, for with his usual bang and clatter Jon arrived breathless at the back door. "Can we have a basin and some paper bags, Mom?" he shouted. "There's simply millions of them—and they're whoppers!"

"Millions of what?" asked Mother. "Ants or caterpillars?"

"Blackberries!" panted Jon. "We could make lots and lots of jam—at least you and Jenny could!"

He fidgeted while Mother searched for paper bags, telling her all about the door in the wall, and how Beth had gone through it again to put the kitten out, and had run up the lane a little way with it.

There, where the lane widened, she had noticed a sprawling blackberry bush which grew against the high wall. Jenny and Jon had found her picking and eating, quite unconcerned that she was in disgrace.

"I'll go and tell Crispin," he said as he finished explaining. "Guess he likes picking blackberries."

He stumped away upstairs to the attic where Crispin had taken refuge, and found him leaning out of the window. Crispin had been trying to cheer himself up by gazing at the castle. But Beth's words, 'you don't belong anywhere,' kept going through his mind. He had been wondering how long it would be before a letter came from New York with instructions about some other awful boarding school. It would be much better, he thought, to stay where he was if the Bernards could put up with him, and if he could stop himself getting angry at Beth.

Before he could decide what to do next time she made him angry, Jon burst in shouting, "Come and see what we've found!" Although he still felt unwanted, curiosity made him go.

Jenny and Beth already had purple mouths and fingers when the boys joined them. It was hot in the lane where the September sunshine beat down on the old walls, and brought out the sweet, tangy smell of the blackberries.

The little tabby kitten, which had refused to go home, skitted about pouncing on dead leaves. "It wants to stay with us," said Jon when he saw it, and found a long grass to tickle it with.

"We've got a bag and a bowl," said Crispin to Jenny, ignoring Beth, who was trying to unhook a bramble from her shorts. Crispin liked eleven-year-old Jenny, with her dark curly hair and sparkling eyes. She was one of the 'bean-pole' kind like Simon, while Beth and Jon were both fair and chubby.

Many of the best berries were out of reach, but Beth solved that problem. She ran back to Sunnyhill and returned with a walking stick. It had a silver handle, Crispin noticed, but Beth hooked down the shining bunches with it in a most casual fashion.

Presently Jon, hearing the kitten rustling about under the big bush, squeezed in beside the wall to coax her out. "You out there! Come and look at this funny thing!"

They heard his excited voice, and Jenny answered, teasing, "Have you found another door?"

To their surprise he called, "Another kind of one—but it's too small for a door—it's a kind of window in the wall with a shutter!"

It was certainly an odd sort of door that Jon had found. In spite of a few scratches they all crowded into the narrow space by the wall to puzzle over the square of old wood in the stonework.

"It's too small for a grown-up to get through," said Beth, "and it's too near the ground to be a window."

Crispin tried to push past Jenny, getting well scratched for his pains. "There's a knothole," he said. "If you put your eye to it you'll see what's on the other side—"

Beth crouched uncomfortably, and tried to follow his advice. "Don't crowd me, Jon! Don't push—I can't see a thing—Oh! Oww—"

There was a sudden creak as she leaned her full

weight on the rotting boards, and then with a crash the shutter fell inwards.

"Oh help! Now you've gone and smashed it!" Jenny tried to sound reproving. But the others pushed forward to look at a long garden which sloped away from them, with great trees half hiding a big old house at the bottom. The wide sweep of lawn had an untended look, and late roses bloomed in tangled flower beds.

Jenny longed to climb through, and stand where the sun shone warmly on a flagstoned path.

Crispin must have read her thoughts. "I'd love an excuse to go down and look at that house," he said, as Jon reached in to try and pick up the fallen boards.

And then their excuse arrived unbidden, for with a little excited meow, the kitten crawled out from the blackberry bush, slipped under Jon's arm, and jumped lightly into the garden.

"That's where he lives!" exclaimed Beth. "But he's an awful long way from the house—and he's so small—"

They looked at each other, and Crispin grinned. "We'll take him home," he said, "we'll apologize about the shutter. The people can't be cross if we take their kitten back."

One by one they climbed through the hole, and saw to their surprise that some old out-buildings stood on the inside of the wall.

"Stables, I guess," said Crispin. "That half-door looks like a horse's stall. But it's a funny place for horses with no gate into the lane."

Jenny didn't answer. She was trying to catch the kitten which ran around in the sunshine. "Help me,

Beth! We can't go down to the house unless we've got it to give back!"

Beth pulled off her headband which kept her long hair off her face, and trailed it invitingly along the ground.

Two minutes later the kitten was captured, and they started to walk rather self-consciously down the long lawn. They were aware that they were in view of all those big, uncurtained windows.

But nobody came out to meet them. They went unchallenged till they reached the steps of a wide terrace, where little pink flowers sprouted between the flagstones, and a tiny lizard lay motionless on the sun-warmed railing.

There was such a stillness about the old place that even Jon didn't bounce about as usual. Jenny had a feeling that some kind of ogre might be lying in wait beyond the French windows.

The muffled roar of traffic told them that the front of the house must face the main street of the town, but here in the garden it was like the palace of the Sleeping Beauty.

"I believe it's empty," began Crispin.

Then suddenly a voice behind them said quietly, "I see I have visitors."

Crispin swung around, and the kitten gave a stifled meow as Beth involuntarily gripped it tighter. A tall elderly man had come unseen along the terrace from a side door, and stood looking down at the four of them with a quizzical smile.

Jenny flushed under his gaze, but found her tongue first. "I—we brought your kitten back—it strayed into our garden, and we didn't know where it lived till it came through the hole—"

"Through the hole?" the old gentleman looked puzzled, and added, "Actually I've never seen the kitten before, but I'm intrigued to know how you got into my garden without coming to the front door!"

"The hole—" said Crispin, feeling that they had made a very big blunder, "the one with the shutter over it, up by your stable. I'm afraid we've broken the shutter, but we didn't mean to—it just gave way when we leaned on it."

"We were picking blackberries really, and I found it," piped up Jon. But Beth stood silent, staring at the tall stranger, and stroking the kitten which trembled under her hand with a rhythmic purr.

"Ah! up by the stable! I haven't had time to find out the lay of the land up there!" With a brief glance towards the top of the garden the man turned and walked along the terrace, beckoning them to follow. At the far end was a long stone seat. "Suppose we sit down and get acquainted," he said. "You see, I only came here a week ago, and I still make new discoveries about the place a dozen times a day."

"We've only just come, too!" exclaimed Beth, suddenly deciding that she liked him. "We moved into the house across the lane last night!"

She sat down on the warm stones at his feet, and made a comfortable lap for the kitten. Crispin perched on the railing, and Jenny shyly took a seat on the bench.

"Didn't you know you had a hole in the wall when you bought the house?" asked Jon, who was jigging about on his heels, unable to sit still, as usual.

"Well, the fact is," said their new acquaintance, "I didn't buy it. It was bequeathed to me by an elderly relative. It's what's called an inheritance."

"Boy! I'd like to be left a place as big as this!" exclaimed Crispin. "Aren't you pleased about it?" And then, without waiting for an answer he added, "What shall we call you, please?"

"My name is Cameron. Yes, I am pleased about the house. But I would be more so if it wasn't quite so dilapidated—it rained the day before yesterday, and the roof is like a sieve in places. The whole house would need a fortune to repair."

Mr. Cameron stretched his long legs, and picked a piece of grass from between the stones to tickle the kitten with. "I think you should tell me who you are," he said, "as we are such near neighbors."

Jenny introduced them. "I'm Jenny, and these are Beth and Jon. There's Simon at home helping Dad and Mother to get settled—he's fourteen."

"And you?" asked Mr. Cameron, looking at Crispin very hard, as he had done several times already.

"I'm Crispin. Crispin Cotterell—I'm just staying—" said Crispin, "I guess I look different from the others."

"Well, of course, there's not a family likeness." Mr. Cameron glanced from one to the other, and then added, "You remind me of someone very strongly, but I know no one by the name of Cotterell."

Beth was just about to tell Crispin's story when Jon changed the subject for them. "This house is as old as old," he announced. "Is it as old as the castle?"

"Of course it isn't, stupid!" said Beth. "I'd have known that even when I was your age!"

"The castle is as old as William the Conqueror, isn't it?" asked Jenny. "Jon isn't doing much history yet," she added, to soothe hurt feelings.

Crispin slipped off the railing, and came to sit on the bench. "Do you know much about it?" he asked eagerly. "I'm dying to go up there!"

"I haven't been up for years," Mr. Cameron told them, "but I used to love it when I was a boy. Yes, Jenny, a lot of it dates from old William—but Henry the Second built the main tower. The Romans had a fort there hundreds of years before that—it's England's history written in stone. They call Dover 'England's Gateway,' you know."

Then, getting up stiffly from the bench, he said, "I came across a book about it yesterday, and a map, too, in the old library here. It might interest you to see them."

"Oh, can we?" asked Jenny. "If we know something about it we can tell Simon—I guess he'll take us after Daddy goes next week."

They followed Mr. Cameron through dusty French windows into a high, book-lined room, and watched fascinated while he wheeled a tall pair of steps to one of the bookcases and climbed up.

A cloud of dust, which made Jenny sneeze, came down with the old brown volume he chose. "Apparently I've inherited the dust of ages as well—" began Mr. Cameron, when there was a tap at the door.

"Ah! Mrs. Mundell," he exclaimed, "come in—I have visitors!" Mrs. Mundell was a large, elderly woman, with her gray hair done up in braids around her head. She looked disapproving, Jenny thought.

Jenny was suddenly conscious that her jeans had a slit in the knee, and that Jon's shirt needed mending.

But Mrs. Mundell was staring at Crispin. Then she looked hard at Mr. Cameron, who nodded slightly as though he understood her thoughts.

"Will you be wanting lunch on the terrace this nice day, Sir?" was all she said.

Mr. Cameron answered hurriedly, "Dear, dear, is it that time already? Can you children come and see this book another day?"

They were all disappointed, but glad that they could come again. "I'm sure Mother will let us," said Jenny, as they were shepherded into the garden. "Thank you for asking us in, as the kitten wasn't yours," she added.

Mr. Cameron chuckled. "He introduced us anyway," he said. "I suggest you go out the way you came in, and leave him in the lane—he'll probably go and find his mother. In fact, there may be a stray cat up in those stables."

"Oh! may we look?" asked Beth. "We'd be awfully careful, and not get into any mischief."

"Go by all means—" Mr. Cameron waved them onto the lawn, aware that Mrs. Mundell was bearing down on him with a laden tray. "You may play up at that end of the garden," he added, "but don't invite any other children through the famous hole—one day I must come up myself and see what's in the stables." His eyes twinkled as he looked at their eager faces. "I suggest that you make a 'preliminary survey'!"

4
Around the Harbor

They hurried up the steep lawn, turning to wave to Mr. Cameron as they neared the top. "I'm hungry!" said Jon. "I'm starving!"

"Me, too." Beth hesitated, as Crispin marched toward the stables.

"Let's come this afternoon," suggested Jenny. "Mother's probably wondering where we are, if dinner's ready."

Crispin was hungry, too. So they put the kitten down by the wall and retrieved their blackberries which they had hidden under the brambles.

"I think Mr. Cameron's super," said Crispin, as Jenny ran to open their garden door. But it was opened for them by Simon.

"You're a fine lot!" he burst out. "Dad sent me to find you ages ago—and you weren't anywhere!"

"Sorry—we forgot about dinner," said Jenny, suddenly contrite. "But Mother and Dad won't mind when they hear where we've been—you just come and listen while we tell."

Dad and Mother were certainly interested in their

morning's adventures, and the expected scolding was forgotten.

"Mr. Cameron sounds like a very nice person," said Mother, as she began second helpings all around. "We seem to have moved into a place full of surprises! And now that we're reasonably settled," she told them, "Daddy has a surprise for you this afternoon. You must have one treat with him before he goes."

"Before he goes where?" asked Crispin, above the clamor of Jon kicking the table leg and shouting, "What are we doing, Daddy? Tell us where we're going."

"Be quiet a minute, Jon, while I answer Crispin—" Mr. Bernard put a restraining hand on his youngest, while he explained, "I'm purser on one of the big liners that sail out of the London Docks. That means I'm away for weeks at a time. So you'll have to help Simon take care of the family generally, Crispin, if you stay here awhile."

Crispin flashed him a grateful look; it was good to be included in the family.

Now Crispin hoped fervently that Mr. Bernard's treat would be to take them to the Castle.

But he was disappointed. "I imagine you're all dying to get on the water," said Mr. Bernard. "So we're going down to the harbor, and I'll get you in some sort of boat—"

The rest of the plan was drowned in shouts of delight, while Mother said hastily, "Not me, Daddy! I just wasn't made for small boats. I'll stay and get the clothes unpacked."

So, half an hour later they were all jammed in Daddy's old car, driving down the busy main street of

Dover, which seemed choked with cars and people returning from holidays abroad. At last they were through to the wide, peaceful sweep of the sea front. When Dad had found a spot to park, they tumbled out and started to explore.

"It's a super place!" decided Simon, delighted by the small yachts, with sails of every color, which skimmed like butterflies across the harbor. There were plenty of swimmers and small canoes, and near the long pier someone on water skis was being towed in a wide arc away from the shore.

"There's a liner coming in! Look—it's a green one!" squeaked Jon.

"That's not a liner! It's a car ferry, isn't it, Dad?" Simon asked a little doubtfully, for the vessel certainly looked very big.

"If it's green," said Mr. Bernard, "it's the *New Enterprise,* one of the ships that takes cars and people over to France. You'll see lots of them, Jon. They come in and out like buses all summer."

Jenny and Beth had gone flying down a concrete pier to watch a boat being winched ashore, and Simon headed in the same direction.

Mr. Bernard looked down at Crispin, who was still beside him. "You like it here?" he asked kindly.

"It's great!" answered Crispin. "It's the best place I've ever been, I think—it's got everything!"

He looked from the sparkling water to the towering white cliffs, and right above them, watching over the town, the castle stood majestic and beautiful.

Mr. Bernard glanced up just as a helicopter came whirring over their heads. "You're right, Crispin—old and new—it's got the best of both worlds. Enjoy it while you can."

Shouts from Simon made them hurry. A group of late holidaymakers was gathering on a wooden pier, while a big motorboat waited with engine running. A man in a blue shirt urged them to 'step lively,' and Beth was jumping around in the shallow water carrying her sandals.

"Here's the boat, Daddy!" she shouted. "You said we could go."

"All around the harbor! Half hour sail!" called blue shirt, and Jon somehow got himself in front of the other people and asked to be lifted in. That settled it. Soon they were all aboard, and chugging out past the yachts, the dredgers, and the Pilot Boat, towards the green, tumbling water of the Channel.

The buildings on the shore looked tiny by the time they reached the great harbor wall which makes a shelter for anchored ships. To Jon's regret, the car ferry had gone into its berth, and they could see nothing but its funnels.

"Never mind," Daddy promised him, "you'll see one close up before you go home."

That mystified them, for the motor boat was turning shorewards. "This way," said Mr. Bernard as they scrambled onto the shore once more. "I'll race you to the pier!"

Simon and Crispin outran him, and Jon came puffing behind them all.

They were only just in time. As Mr. Bernard bought their pier tickets a brown mini-bus came trundling along, and turned around to wait for them.

"I didn't know they had buses on piers!" panted Beth, as Simon pushed her in. "What are we going in this for, Daddy? We'll only see what we saw from the boat!"

"This time you're going to see it from a lighthouse," she was told, and when they had driven down the long, long pier, past all the people fishing with rod and line, they found another treat in store for them.

They crowded up the steps which led into the old lighthouse. An ancient ship's figurehead of a woman, with her blue dress seeming to ripple in the breeze, looked down at them from the wall. The salt air blew cold out there, and made Beth shiver. But soon she was warm, for the top of the lighthouse was a café, with people chattering at little red tables, and looking at the crowded harbor out of huge windows.

"I didn't know I was hungry, but now I could eat and eat!" said Jenny.

Simon and Daddy had just arrived with loaded trays, when Jon gave a great shout. "It's here! Look! Look! I could touch it!"

And suddenly a ship came so close to them that it seemed as if it might ram the pier. So close it was that people on the deck waved to Jon as he leaned out of the window, with Jenny clutching him around the waist in case he fell. In a second they were all looking out to wave as the vessel slid past, with the gulls swooping and crying in her white wake.

Jon was so excited that in spite of hunger he could hardly settle down to eat. "I want to go on one of those big ones, Daddy—when can I?" he asked.

But before her father could answer, Beth cut in.

"You'd be sick as soon as you got out in the rough water! You're always sick on anything that goes up and down because you're just a silly little boy."

Jon flushed, and the happy look faded from his face.

"Beth," said Dad sternly, "there was no need to say that. You used to be sick yourself when you were little. One day you'll be sorry after you've said some unkind thing, and wish you could unsay it."

"But it's true!" protested Beth.

Crispin looked out to sea, thinking what a nice family the Bernards would be if Beth was not one of them. And then he was aware that Mr. Bernard was looking at Beth so steadily, that in spite of her stubborn frown, the tears were beginning to well up in her eyes.

"You must go straight to your room when we get home," Mr. Bernard was saying, "and bring me your Bible. Find the Epistle of James, Chapter 3, and read the first half of it to me. I shall want you to learn part of it by heart. It may help you not to hurt yourself and others one day in a way that you could not imagine. Now, eat up, all of you. It's time we got back to Mother."

Even Simon looked quite startled. It was unusual for Dad to bring the Bible into any kind of punishment. He always wanted his children to read it with interest, and to find help and comfort in it.

"I didn't know there was a letter by a James in the Bible anyway," thought Crispin, and decided he would look it up and see what Mr. Bernard meant.

Beth was unusually quiet on the way home, but Jon was quite happy again. Dad took them around by the inner harbor, the 'basin' as he called it, and when the car bumped over the cobblestones of the old wharf Jon begged him to stop so that they could have a better look.

They scrambled out of the car and walked along the wharf, stepping over mooring ropes, and going around the stone posts, sniffing the tarry, salty smell of the place.

There were dozens of sailing yachts moored close together in that sheltered spot, which was right in between the houses. Their hulls, painted in every bright color imaginable, were reflected in the mirror-still water, and their tall masts stood like a forest.

Beyond were little old shops and cafés, ships' supply stores, and clothing stores which sold yachting caps and oilskins.

Jenny turned to Crispin and saw he was thrilled with it all. "And your castle is still there!" she said, looking up at the great battlements above them.

"I'd like to be down here at night!" exclaimed Simon. "It must look great with all the lights on."

"Next time I'm home it will be dark early," said his father, "and we'll bring Mother down to see it."

That night, as Crispin climbed up the noisy stairs to the attic, wondering how long it would be before the stair carpet was down, he saw that the door of the girls' room was open. Jenny sat on the bed with her small Bible on her lap, her forehead creased in a frown.

There was no sign of Beth, and he guessed she was with her father. As he went by, Jenny looked up. "I've found it," she said, "come and see—it's pretty fierce!"

Crispin went to look over her shoulder. He read for himself the stern old words about the great ships that are turned with a very small rudder. "Like the car ferries we saw," he said, and read aloud, "'so the tongue is a little member and boasteth great things—the tongue is a fire—the tongue no man can tame—' I say, Jenny, will Beth understand this? She's a lot younger than us!"

"Dad will explain it to her," said Jenny, closing the Bible with a sigh. "It means that the small nasty things we say can do an awful lot of harm, and start big things going wrong. A small fire can grow and burn down a house, and Beth's tongue is a fire sometimes—she means it to hurt, and it burns up other people's happiness. Don't let her hurt you, Crispin."

"I won't," said Crispin firmly. "She can say what she likes, but she won't hurt me." But Jenny, looking at the set line of his mouth guessed that Crispin could be hurt very much.

5

Mr. Crump Takes a Hand

The next morning a letter from Aunt Anthea arrived, mailed just before she flew to New York. Daddy read it at breakfast, and Crispin watched him with an awful sinking feeling. He was enjoying himself, and now he was probably going to be uprooted again.

But when Mr. Bernard finished reading he looked up with a smile. "It seems we are to have Crispin for a little longer," he said. "Aunt Anthea has been asked to extend her tour of America for four months. She has a boarding school in Italy in mind for you, Crispin, but she can't settle matters just now. She wonders if you could be at school in Dover till Christmas—would you like that?"

"Oh yes, PLEASE!" cried Crispin, nearly upsetting the milk jug in his joy, and then looking quickly at Mrs. Bernard to see if she was pleased, too.

Her eyes met his with a smile that was so warm and friendly that he suddenly felt as light as air. Simon and Jenny both said, "Good!" but Beth gave Crispin a long stare, and made a face.

"I won't let her spoil it for me—I won't!" he thought fiercely. After breakfast the whole house was filled with the delicious smell of blackberries cooking. Mother was making jam. Simon and Dad prepared to put down the stair carpet. It seemed as though the others could do what they liked, once the breakfast things were washed up.

"Let's go and see those stables!" said Jenny. "Let's take some cake crumbs in case the kitten's around."

They ran down the garden path and past the big round patch of ashes where their bonfire had been. They found the old door easy to open, because Simon had oiled the hinges.

Soon they were all behind the blackberry bush, though Jon, who came last was somewhat scratched, because a boy came bicycling along the lane and Jon was afraid of being seen.

The door to the main stable was padlocked, but the stall Crispin had noticed had a half door of slats. These had rotted with wind and weather, and it was easy to push one aside and reach in to slide the bolt.

"Poof! It smells musty!" exclaimed Beth, wrinkling her nose as Crispin led them in. Jenny wished there was still a horse to fondle and feed with sugar as they saw the empty manger, and the old iron drinking trough.

"There's a door into the locked part," announced Jon. But the others were too busy looking at a stack of old, dust-covered trunks which had been stored in the empty stall for more years than they could guess.

"They all belonged to someone called 'Charles Curtis Cameron'." Crispin looked at the neat lettering on tattered labels, and Beth lifted the heavy lid of one.

"Empty!" she said, and let it drop, sending up a cloud of dust which made them all sneeze.

"Come and look what's in here!" Jon's excited shout came from the harness room and hay loft beyond. It was dim there, with thin beams of light filtering through the shuttered windows.

They found Jon mounted high on a pile of hay bales, with more rising up like a wall behind him, till they nearly touched the ceiling. "We could make some castles," he announced. "We could make hay forts and play cowboys and Indians!" He fired an imaginary pistol into the air with an ear-splitting yell.

"You mind you don't topple," Jenny told him. "You'd better jump, and let me catch you."

But Jon was in no mood to be caught. He bounced up and down, sending showers of moldy hay down on the others. "There's a door up over my head," he told them, "and there's a ladder behind this wall of hay — I can just see the top of it!"

"I believe you're right! There's a trap door up there—hold still Jon, I'm coming up—"

Crispin climbed the mountain of hay bales with more caution than Jon had done. Jenny watched him with a puzzled expression. "Funny, having all this hay," she said, "when they couldn't have had more than two horses. And funny not having a gate into the lane. There doesn't seem any way into the main street except through the house either."

But she didn't have any time to work out the puzzle, for Jon, who had backed away to make room for Crispin, suddenly lost his balance.

He came tumbling down to land with a bump at Jenny's feet.

"Oh Jon! Are you hurt? I told you to be careful—"

began Jenny, as he sat up and his mouth went square, ready for a howl of woe.

But at that moment they were all startled by the sound of heavy feet in the stall. Beth, who was fiddling with some stiff old harness, swung around in time to be caught by a horny hand.

"You little good for nothing varmints!" roared a cracked old voice. "I'll teach you to come meddling and trespassing! Come out of it, all of you!"

In the dim light they saw a sturdy old man, who looked large and terrifying as he swooped down on the unlucky Jon, and jerked him to his feet.

"Come on!" he roared again. "You come along o'me!"

As Crispin jumped down to protest, and Jenny tried to rescue Jon, who howled afresh, he hauled the two younger children out into the sunlight, and began marching them down the lawn.

"We weren't trespassing! We had permission!" cried Crispin running after him.

Jenny pleaded, "Do let go of Jon's ear—you're hurting him terribly, and we weren't doing any harm!"

They were nearly down to the house before the angry old man looked around. Jenny guessed he was a gardener. They had just reached the terrace steps when he turned to see if Jenny was following, and his eyes met Crispin's blazing blue ones.

He stopped so suddenly that Beth nearly fell over. He stared at Crispin with a look of absolute astonishment. At that moment the French windows opened, and Mr. Cameron came out.

"What's happening?" he asked sharply. "What have

Jon and Beth done to be hauled about like this? Is anything wrong, Crump?"

It was Mr. Crump's turn to look crestfallen. He let go of Jon's ear and Beth's shirt hurriedly.

"Found them trespassing in the stables, Zir," he mumbled. "Didn't know they was friends of yours."

"Well, you know now," said Mr. Cameron. "They have my full permission to play in the stables if they wish, but of course you were right to challenge them. You had better come indoors, children. Jon seems to be somewhat the worse for wear."

The old man stumped off muttering, as Mr. Cameron led the way into the library. But he turned and gave Crispin a long look as he went, "as though he'd seen a ghost," Crispin said afterwards.

"Mr. Crump is going to get the garden shipshape for me on Wednesdays and Thursdays," Mr. Cameron told the others, when Jon had gone off with Mrs. Mundell to have his face washed. "He's a crusty old man if you rub him the wrong way. But gardeners are hard to get, and he used to work here many years ago."

"Has Mrs. Mundell been here a long time, too?" Jenny asked, finding a seat on the broad windowsill.

"Since she was a girl," Mr. Cameron answered. "She came as parlormaid in the days when big houses kept a lot of servants, and it's been her only home ever since. That's why I shall be sorry to sell the old place if I have to."

"Sell it?" exclaimed Crispin. "Aren't you going to stay here, now it's yours?"

"I'd like to," he answered sadly, "but I'm afraid that unless I spend more on it than I can afford, the whole place will tumble about my ears. Nothing has been repaired for twenty years. My old uncle wouldn't have workmen around, and he only used a few of the rooms. Mrs. Mundell has kept the kitchen and the housekeeper's room cosy of late, but that's about all."

"And we've only just met you!" said Beth unexpectedly. "It'll be horrid if you go away."

"Cheer up!" Mr. Cameron laughed. "I haven't sold it yet! Crump tells me that my uncle, when he was getting old and ill, was always talking about having a treasure somewhere. Perhaps I'll come across it! Then I promise you I shall get the builders in to repair the roof!"

Jon returned at that moment eating an apple and looking clean again. Behind him came Mrs. Mundell with a tray of lemonade and gingerbread, which cheered Jenny considerably. "Anyway she must like us better than Mr. Crump does," she thought, as Crispin passed it around. Beth found a place beside her on the windowsill while they ate, and told Mr. Cameron about the lighthouse.

"Now you'll have to see the castle," he said, to Crispin's joy. "I wonder if your parents would let me take you up there myself—I should like to see the old place again after all these years—"

"Great!" shouted Crispin. "I've been aching to go inside ever since I saw it out of the attic window—it was all lighted up the night I came!"

"I believe it's lighted up at night all the year around," Mr. Cameron told them. "If you're fond of history you'll find a lot to enjoy—the armor alone is worth the climb up the hill!"

"Swords and helmets and things?" asked Beth, starting on her second piece of gingerbread.

"All the lot," he told her, "spears, pistols, battle-axes!"

"Is there a breastplate of righteousness?" asked Jon suddenly.

Jenny smothered a giggle, and Beth started to laugh, and then stopped and bit her lip.

"She's remembering what Daddy told her last night I guess," thought Jenny with relief.

Mr. Cameron smiled at Jon and answered, quite unruffled, "No, I don't think you'll find it there. You mean the one St. Paul talked about, don't you? That's a kind of breastplate we can all wear, but other people can't see we've got it on. They only know by the way we behave—"

"Put on the whole armor of God," quoted Crispin. "I learned that once, but I've forgotten most of it."

"It's worth looking up again," Mr. Cameron told him kindly. "You'll find it in Ephesians, chapter six, I believe—it's something we all need to remember when life gets tough."

He reached down the book about Dover Castle, and opened it on the table for them to look at. There was a quaint old map showing the tower and walls, with dates beside them which Crispin found fascinating.

"That stubby little tower by the Church inside the walls is called the old Roman Pharos—" Mr. Cameron pointed it out with his long bony finger. "It was a lighthouse, and it's probably the oldest building standing above ground in the whole of Britain," he told them. "Lots of Roman pavements and villas are found buried underground in places, but this old tower has stood up to all the wind and weather for nearly two thousand years—it was built in A.D. 54."

He stopped a moment to let it sink in, and then he added, "If that doesn't mean a lot to you, you can remember that it was built about the time that St. Paul was writing the letter about the 'breastplate of righteousness.'"

"Wow!" breathed Crispin.

Jenny looked at Mr. Cameron wide-eyed. "Two thousand years!" she said in an awed voice. "Can we really go inside it?"

"This afternoon, if your parents will agree. Suppose I come up and call on them just before lunch? I shall have to go around by the road, because I can't see myself crawling under a blackberry bush! I'm surprised that there isn't a gate up there. I must ask Crump if he knows anything about it."

The children were thrilled at his offer. "Daddy has to go to his ship tomorrow," said Jenny, "and I know he'd like to meet you first. He said it was nice to know a neighbor so soon, expecially someone old. I mean—" she added, flushing, "I mean someone grown up—not just children—"

"I know just what you mean—even if you weren't exactly diplomatic!" he answered, his eyes twinkling under their bushy brows. "Run home now and leave me to write letters—you can explore the stable again another day."

They scampered up the lawn, giving a wide berth to Mr. Crump, who was digging weeds out of a flowerbed. "We won't come back till Friday, when he isn't here," said Beth. "He'd be sure to come prowling around and spoil it—"

"I spy something!" called Jon, as he reached the hole. "I spy the stripey kitten up on the wall!"

But with Mr. Crump's eyes upon them they didn't stop to coax it down. Beth pulled the bag of cake crumbs out of her pocket. "I'll leave it by the blackberry bush," she said. "If he's hungry he'll find it—let's hurry and ask Mother about this afternoon!"

Crispin felt as excited as if he had had three birthdays all rolled into one. To go to the Castle with Mr. Cameron who knew so much seemed almost too good to be true. "Dreams do come true sometimes!" he said to himself as they ran home down the lane. He went straight upstairs to the attic room and leaned out of the window. "That stubby little tower by the church—" he thought, gazing at the sunlit Castle. "It must have stood up there by itself for centuries when there was no Dover at all—only wild green hills. It's waited all this time for me to come and find it!"

6

The Castle at Last

Both their parents were delighted at Mr. Cameron's offer. "It's very kind of him to want to take five children," said Mother, "but you'll learn a lot more about it than if you went by yourselves—"

"Am I supposed to go, too?" asked Simon, who didn't like being called a child, and Beth answered, "Wait till you're asked!"

She ran out with Jon and Crispin after the clock in the hall struck twelve to see if Mr. Cameron was coming up from the bottom of the lane. There was no one in sight, not even the kitten, but Jon soon found a new entertainment.

Several of the garden doors on the slope of the hill were set low in the ground, and there were steps going down to them. These had an iron rail to prevent people from falling down the steps as they walked along the lane on dark nights.

"I can do a roll over and over—" announced Jon, seizing the nearest rail and swinging over on his stomach. He hung for a moment head downwards, but, try as he would, he couldn't make the complete turn. He dropped down on the steps grumbling in disgust.

"I can do that!" said Beth promptly, and did so. But she came over too far, and fell on her back, making a black mark on her shorts.

"Let's see if I can—get out of the way a minute, Jon—" Crispin was poised upside down for a moment, and in that second something slipped from the neck of his T-shirt and dangled on a thin chain.

With an effort he swung right over and landed on his feet again, but Beth's quick eyes had seen the flash of silver as he quickly stuffed it back. "You're wearing a necklace!" she said. "It's a locket, isn't it? Only babies wear lockets. I'll tell Simon and he'll laugh!"

"It's not a locket and it's none of your business!" Crispin flushed up to the ears, and his blue eyes flashed.

But Beth wasn't going to leave it at that. "Lucy, Lucy Locket!" she sang, dancing around Crispin, who glared at her.

Jon dodged in front of Beth. "You're horrible!" he spluttered. "You know what Daddy said!"

"What's going on?" Mr. Cameron's voice startled them. "Have I arrived in the middle of an argument?"

Beth stopped dancing, and Crispin turned to him with relief. "It's nothing, Sir," he said, "we were only squabbling."

Jon raced ahead to their garden door calling, "I'll go and tell Daddy you've come!"

Mr. Cameron seemed at home right away at Sunnyhill. He settled into one of the deep armchairs and chatted to Dad so long that Mother tried to persuade him to stay to lunch.

But Mrs. Mundell was expecting him back, so, reluctantly, they all escorted him out into the garden again.

As he shook hands with Mr. Bernard he said warmly, "If I find that I can stay in Dover and make it my home I shall enjoy it all the more because of knowing you—but I'm afraid that depends on the builder's estimate."

It was another golden afternoon as they climbed the steep path to the castle from where the bus let them off. The great walls towered above them as they crossed the dry moat by a sturdy bridge, to go in under the dark archway called the Constable's Gate.

They went slowly, because every few steps they simply had to turn and look down the thick wooded slopes to the town and harbor so very far below.

There was a silvery haze over it all in the bright sunlight, and crows sailed out from the castle walls and circled in the still air over that breathtaking drop.

"It's like being on top of a mountain," said Jon, who tugged at Jenny's hand to make her look at everything. Certainly the *New Enterprise* sailing out of the harbor looked like a tiny toy from where they stood.

"The Romans picked a fine place to build when first they made a fort up here," said Mr. Cameron, "but I don't envy their British slaves who had to drag all the massive stones for it up this enormous hill!"

"The Romans didn't build this, did they?" asked Beth, as they went into the shadow of the great gateway, with its iron gate drawn up, high above them in the darkness.

"No, nor any of what we see now, I think, except the Pharos lighthouse tower," Mr. Cameron told her. "Parts of the castle have been built and added to for centuries, but King Henry the Second did most of it. Lots of the great men who were Constables of the Castle from early times had parts of fortification done. We'll find a list of them inside somewhere, I believe. It begins I know with Godwin, Earl of Kent, in ten hundred and something, and it ends with Sir Winston Churchill, and now—"

"I never cared much about history," murmured Simon, tilting his head to gaze up at the tower, "but this certainly makes it come alive!"

For the next three hours they wandered and looked. They saw the great well, and marvelled at its enormous depth. They climbed spiral staircases and came out at last on top of the tower beside the flagstaff, from which the Union Jack flag floated out above their heads.

Mr. Cameron took a photograph of them all clustered by the turret door. "To remember a happy day by," he said.

Jon's legs began to ache long before they had seen all the armor. He looked out of dozens of tiny slits made to shoot arrows through if invaders came up the hill. Crispin kept straying away to see things by himself. He was blissfully happy, and wished they could stay for days instead of hours.

"I think we need something to eat," said Mr. Cameron at last.

"I saw a notice which said RESTAURANT!" announced Beth eagerly. "I'm just starving, and my legs won't go another step!"

So they trooped down, and followed other hungry sightseers to find Beth's restaurant, tucked away behind the tower.

"This is what I call good food!" Simon attacked a huge plate of sausages, eggs, and potatoes, as though he had been one of the old defenders of the castle, just released from a siege.

"I like being me—now—" said Jon, "the Romans didn't have baked beans—"

"Nor fizzy lemonade!" Beth giggled.

Mr. Cameron laughed, and looked at Jenny. "Why so thoughtful?" he asked, seeing that she was eating slowly with what Simon called her 'faraway look.'

"I was thinking," she replied, coming back to the present abruptly, "about that little chapel we found up in the tower. People must have gone to church in the castle for hundreds of years—"

Mr. Cameron nodded. "Up there, and in the other church behind the Pharos. They called that one 'St. Mary de Castro'—it's got a fascinating story. Druids had a pagan temple there long before Julius Caesar and his legions came. Then, many, many years later, when the Romans began to allow the local people to rule themselves, there was a King of Kent called Lucian—"

"And he lived up here?" asked Crispin eagerly.

Their old friend nodded. "He did more than that," he said. "Some very early missionaries came all the way across Italy, and France, and they landed here to tell the people about Jesus Christ. They stayed here with the King for a while, and he decided to become a Christian."

"So he built the church?" asked Jenny. "Is it really as old as that?"

"That one we see now isn't, but a little one was built as long ago as the year one hundred and eighty, right next door to the Pharos. That was long before St. Augustine came."

Simon finished the last of his sausages, and felt free to join in the discussion. "Didn't the Roman soldiers pull out and leave us just about then?" he asked.

"They did," answered Mr. Cameron, "but the Kings of Kent went on ruling, and one called Ethelbert sailed across the Channel and persuaded a French Princess to marry him—and she was a Christian. Perhaps it was she who asked Augustine to come. Anyway he landed here, and went to Canterbury to found his church there. Pour me some more tea, Jenny. I think Beth and Jon look a bit restive—they've probably had enough history for one day!" The café tables were emptying fast.

Simon looked at his watch. "Guess this place will be closing before long," he said, and they went out again into the courtyard.

The long shadows of the evening were falling across it as they turned towards the Constable's Gate. The four Bernard children raced on through the darkness of the archway and down the sunlit path beyond, but Crispin went slowly, beside Mr. Cameron.

"It's been great!" he said, and added with a sigh, "I wish I belonged here, and wasn't always moving around. It would be nice to belong."

The old man looked down at him kindly. "I think I understand," he said. "Mr. Bernard told me a little about you when I was alone with him for awhile this morning. The lady who adopted you seems a very energetic person."

"She didn't adopt me properly," Crispin answered quickly. "She just pays people to look after me. If we had a real home and she stayed there I could love her, but I'm just something extra she's collected—."

There was a quiver in his voice, and Mr. Cameron put a hand on his shoulder. "You know," he said, "you belong to someone who loves you better than even a real mother or father could. Don't bother about Simon and Jenny—they'll wait for us—they're throwing stones into the moat."

"Tell me then," Crispin asked. They leaned on the wall beside the drawbridge, with the evening sun warm on their faces.

"You remember," said Mr. Cameron, "that we were talking about King Lucian a while ago—"

"The first King who was a Christian?"

"Yes, that's right—from his time on, boys and girls who lived on this hill became Christians, too. They would have gone through a lot of hard times, you know. They had to be prepared to die for their faith because the pagan people didn't like them. And then later—much later, after this great tower was built in Norman times, boys like you would have been pages here. They would have been brought up in the Christian faith, knowing they belonged to God. Lots of them must have leaned on this very wall, and dreamed of the day when they could join the Crusades, and ride out beside some knight who had the Cross of Christ on his shield—"

"I'd sure like to have been a Crusader!" exclaimed Crispin.

"Well, you can be something even better. You can join that great company who know that they belong to Jesus Christ, and who have asked Him to take them into His service. You can look up Paul's letter to the Ephesians to find out what weapons He will give you to fight with—I think you know the beginning of that verse already, 'Put on the whole armor of God—'"

Crispin didn't answer. He cupped his chin in his hand and looked out over the harbor, deep in thought. Down on the path below them the others were still busy with their game.

"If you know you belong to God, and ask Jesus Christ to help you in all the battles of life, you are never alone any more," Mr. Cameron told him gently. "You 'belong' in the very best way, and you are safe and secure in His love, which doesn't change. Think about it, laddie. He needs Crusaders in the world today—boys, and girls too, who will take a stand against cruelty, and selfishness, and meanness. Believe in Him, Crispin, and you can be certain He will care for you, in this life—and the next."

"But how can I know that I 'belong'?" asked Crispin, his eyes still on the far horizon.

"Ask Him to accept you, and you'll know," was the answer. "Choose your own time and place and then try to serve Him all your life long. You have seen letters marked O.H.M.S.—official ones?"

"Yes, it means 'On Her Majesty's Service,'" answered Crispin promptly.

"That's right. When you belong to God you are 'On HIS Majesty's Service' and you will want to go out to help lonely, sick, and hungry people in the name of the King of Kings!"

A shout from Jon made them change the subject, and they strolled down to see what the excitement was about. "Look!" called Beth. "We've been trying to hit that big white stone in the middle of the moat, and Jon is the first to do it! Even Simon couldn't!"

"You can try if you like," said Jon, who was enormously proud of himself. Crispin bent down to find a suitable pebble. As he did so Beth bent down, too, and her long hair brushed his face as she whispered, "I can see your pretty locket again—baby!"

Crispin straightened up with a jerk, pushing the silver chain out of sight. Delibertaely he turned his back on her, and aimed his pebble, which fell short, to Jon's delight.

He had no time to try again for Mr. Cameron exclaimed suddenly, "My camera! I clean forgot it! I must have left it in the tearoom—"

"I'll get it!" volunteered Crispin, glad of the excuse. "I'll have to dash, or they'll be closed!"

He turned and raced back across the bridge, past the last visitors as they left the tower. He was furious with Beth, but somehow Mr. Cameron's words had given him a comfortable feeling he had never known before.

7
The Arrow Slit

Crispin arrived panting at the doors of the Castle Restaurant, thankful to find that one or two customers were still there.

"You're just in time!" the smiling girl behind the counter told him. "I noticed the camera beside the table you were sitting at, when I cleared it."

Crispin thanked her, and put the thick leather strap of the camera case around his neck. The weight of it pressed against the silver chain which fascinated Beth so much, and as he ran out past the tower he shifted the camera to make it more comfortable.

His thoughts were racing even faster than his feet. How dare Beth tease him when she was so much younger? Why did he bother about her anyway? And if he did what Mr. Cameron suggested, would it help him not to flare up in a temper, and not to tell lies to get himself out of trouble sometimes?

He was thinking so hard that it was only when he ran under an archway that he realized he was on the wrong path. This arch wasn't nearly as big as the Constable's Gate, and there was no bridge, only the path beside the walls going on ahead of him.

He stopped a moment, bewildered. On the stonework above him a notice said 'Peverell's Tower.' He guessed that the moat must be on the other side of the massive wall which bordered the path, so he reasoned that if he turned back and followed close beside it, he would come to the right archway.

He ran on a few yards to make certain that there was no other way, and then he recognized something they had all seen that afternoon. A narrow slit, taller than himself, made in the wall by builders long ago so that they could shoot down at invaders as they stormed across the moat. Jon had been fascinated by it, and happy to stand there and look down at the tremendous drop, secure in the knowledge that he couldn't possibly fall through.

"I know we passed this, because he wanted to throw something down," thought Crispin, and at that moment another idea struck him. If he were to get rid of his silver chain, Beth would no longer have any reason to torment him. Perhaps, too, she was right. Perhaps it was babyish to wear it still, though it had never seemed so, because it was the only possession which had been really his.

He hitched the camera strap aside, and pulled the chain over his head. From it dangled a thin little silver box, which gave a faint rattle as he held it. It was very old, and badly dented. It had been fastened to the chain by the simple method of punching a hole in it at one corner, and slipping the links through.

For a moment Crispin forgot the camera, and the others waiting impatiently for his return. He had no idea what the little box was intended for, or why it had the faint letters 'C.C.C.' engraved on one side of it. He only knew he had never been without it. An anxious rescuer had found it wound around his tiny arm when he was lifted from the debris of an earthquake long ago.

Aunt Anthea had told him that much. She had said that he was such a fair, blue-eyed baby that an English nurse at the hospital to which he was taken had a special interest in him. As the weeks went by and no one had claimed him, the time had come when he must be given a name. The nurse had suggested her own last name 'Cotterell,' and they had called him 'Crispin Charles' because of the three 'C's' on the silver box.

He glanced to see if there was anyone around, but only the sound of pigeons cooing in the great trees below the Pharos broke the silence.

Suddenly he made up his mind, stepped forward, and threw the tiny box out through the narrow slit. The light caught the flash of silver as it curved downwards, and when he pressed his face against the stonework he could see it dangling far below. It was caught on a tiny bush which grew out from the steep grassy side of the moat. "Well, no one will ever get you up from there, unless it's the crows!" he said aloud. Then, feeling half afraid because of what he had done, he raced back under Peverell's tower.

Seeing some hikers with knapsacks coming downhill from the tower, he gladly followed them, and a moment later he saw the Constable's Gate.

"You were simply ages! What have you been up to?" called Simon even before he joined them. But Mr. Cameron was delighted to see his camera safe, and asked no questions.

When they scrambled aboard the bus, the old man took the back seat beside Crispin.

"I was thinking of the conversation we had just now," he said, when the others had trooped up to take the front seats. "I know that you were found after a disaster somewhere abroad, but was there nothing near you, or on your clothes, to give a clue as to who you are?"

Crispin was startled. The guilty feeling about throwing away the silver box made him feel a little sick, but he answered quickly, "No—no—nothing—"

Then the thought came to him that the knights of old, who wore the red cross on their shields, would surely have learned to be truthful, and he muttered desperately, "Anyway—there's nothing now!"

Perhaps the noise of the bus prevented Mr. Cameron from hearing that, because he just said, "Pity—a great pity—" and changed the subject.

It was nearly bedtime for Jon by the time Mr. Cameron said good night, and the children crowded out to the kitchen while Mother made their mugs of cocoa.

"It was wonderful this afternoon!" said Jenny, perched, starry-eyed, on the edge of the kitchen table. "D'you know, Dad, Charles the First waited at the bottom of the castle staircase for his Queen Henrietta to come down it in all her bridal things for their wedding—"

"Big fat Henry—you know, the one who beheaded his wives—he built the first decent pier for Dover Harbor!" put in Beth, reaching for a biscuit.

Simon gulped his cocoa, and made for the back door. "I'm going to fix my bike, Mom," he called as he went out, and added, "We could see France from up there—If I'd had your binocs, Dad, we could have picked out the fields!"

"Then it's going to rain pretty soon," said his father. "When you can see that far it's always a sign."

"Oh, it can't!" said Jon. "It's nearly the end of vacation—it's just GOT to stay fine till next week!"

Jenny laughed. "Come on, Pieface," she said, "I'll come and scrub your knees for you. We'll do something good tomorrow whether it rains or not."

"Tomorrow," thought Crispin to himself, "I'm going to try and be the sort of Crusader that Mr. Cameron talked about, and not tell any lies at all—that is, if it's not too hard."

The next morning they woke to a gentle drizzle, and when Crispin looked out of his window he found that the castle had completely vanished, lost in a bank of low cloud which hid the great hills completely.

"Let's explore that stable place, Jenny. That'll be dry," suggested Jon as they finished breakfast.

But Beth said quickly, "We can't! It's Thursday; that old grumpy Crump will be there and spoil it for us."

"I'm afraid you'll have to find something to do indoors. Clear these things away for me, Jenny. I have to help Daddy pack—"

Mother went upstairs with a step that wasn't as light as usual. They all hated the days when Mr. Bernard went back to his ship.

Crispin drifted aimlessly around while Jenny and Beth washed the dishes. They had declined his help. Simon had disappeared on some mysterious errand of his own. Crispin had just discovered an old Schoolboy's

Annual and was idly flipping over the pages, when there came a call from the front door.

"Who's had my silver-topped walking stick? It's not in the umbrella stand!"

Mr. Bernard sounded ruffled. Crispin followed Jenny and Beth into the hall. "Well?" asked Mr. Bernard, as Jon stumped downstairs. "Who knows where it is? You know you're not supposed to play with it—it was your Grandad's."

Jenny looked at Beth, but Beth put her hands in her pockets, and shook her long hair back on her shoulders. "I haven't a clue where it is," she said sweetly, "but Jon had it on Tuesday—"

Crispin was surprised. Often and often he'd told untruths, or half truths to crotchety schoolmasters, or French policemen who had discovered him up to mischief, but to blame it on little Jon!

"It wasn't Jon's fault!" said Jenny quickly.

Jon turned to Beth, his small face red, between anger and tears. "I didn't! I didn't! You know I didn't get it!"

But Beth remained unmoved. "I didn't say you got it, I just said you HAD it—" she began loftily, but her father cut her short.

"Whoever got it, or had it, knew perfectly well they shouldn't touch it!" he said gruffly. "I've got to go now, but if that stick isn't in its place when I get home—"

He didn't say what he would do, but kissed them all, and hurried to the car. Mother came running downstairs to say good-by. Sensing a quarrel about to begin over the walking stick, Crispin said quickly, "Come on—I'll help you find it. It must be by the blackberries somewhere."

In the end they all trooped down the garden in their mackintoshes, and out into the lane. They hunted around the dripping blackberry bush, and wet nettles soaked the tops of their boots, but there was no sign of the walking stick.

Even Beth began to look frightened, and Jenny said anxiously, "Anyone might pick it up because it had a silver top, but I'm sure we had it when Jon found the hole, and I can't remember putting it down."

"Did anyone take it through the hole?" asked Crispin. "I'm sure I didn't."

Jon rubbed his chin with a dirty finger. "I tried to hook the pussy with it," he said, "when we were catching him—inside—"

"That means we've just got to go in. Perhaps old Crumpy's got it already," said Beth, and began to squeeze into the narrow space by the wall. "I can hear something!" said Beth suddenly. "It's something crying—very small—"

Jenny's dark eyes widened as she listened, too. "It's the kitten!" she exclaimed. "It's hurt I believe, or it wouldn't cry like that—wherever can it be?"

8

The Kitten and a Rescue

They crawled through the hole faster than they had ever done before, and there, just on the other side, lying by a straggly clump of phlox, was the walking stick. "Goody!" exclaimed Beth, pouncing on it, but the others were standing listening anxiously for the piteous little cry.

It came again, high above their heads, and looking up Crispin caught a movement at the gable end of the old stable.

"There! There it is!" he exclaimed. "You can see its face inside that dirty little window! It's got in somehow and it's probably starving!"

"That's the loft up there," said Beth. "I can't think how it got there because the trap door thing in the ceiling was shut."

"We'll find out!" Crispin ran to the stable, and found the main door ajar. "This way!" he said, but got no further. The door wouldn't budge another inch. There was a new padlock on the stall door so that way was barred.

"I'll push," said Jenny. "It's probably stiff."

"There's something on the inside, blocking it," Crispin told her, putting his eye to the small gap.

"Hay!" said Jenny. "The hay's fallen against it—we'll have to—" She stopped suddenly, for from inside the stable came a muffled moan, and a horrible choking sound.

For a second they all stood still, unable to move. Then Jon clutched at Jenny and pulled her from the door. "I'm scared!" he whispered. "There's a THING in there—I'm going home!"

Beth backed away, too, but Crispin said, "It's a person, and he's hurt! We've just got to get in—it might be Mr. Cameron—"

Then even Jon forgot to be afraid, and they all pushed at the door till slowly it began to yield. "I can squeeze in," said Beth bravely. "I'll get around and shove the bales."

A moment later she was inside, pushing at the musty smelling hay. The 'hay wall' they had seen the day before had fallen, and mounds of it filled the stable floor. From somewhere underneath it the moaning began again.

"Come on—quickly!" gasped Beth as the door creaked wider, and the other three forced their way in. Light streamed down on them from above, for the trap door was wide open, and a sturdy ladder was below it.

Jon pointed upwards. "The kitty! I can see him!"

Jenny glanced up, and saw the small face looking down from the edge of the hole. "It's afraid to come down—we'll get it presently, Jon," she said, and joined Crispin, who had scrambled towards the far wall where he could see a boot sticking out from the mound of fodder.

Together they pulled and tugged, and then to their joy they saw a movement under the hay. As they scrabbled away the last armsful a red face came into view. It was Mr. Crump.

He stared at the children for a moment or two, and then began to sneeze.

"Can you sit up?" asked Jenny, beginning to giggle in spite of herself, for he certainly looked peculiar, with a kind of crown of hay sticking to his bald head.

Crispin fought back his laughter, too, because the poor old man seemed very shaken. Somehow they dragged him up and got him sitting on a bale. Blood flowed from a cut behind his ear, and a big bruise was darkening on his cheek. "Them old bales of hay, they was rotten—" he gasped, "crumpled under me they did as I stepped back off that ladder. There's a cat somewheres and it startled me—can't abide cats—"

"It's only a little tiny kitten," Beth told him scornfully. "It's got up in the loft and it can't get down!"

Tactfully Jenny began to brush the hay off Mr. Crump's shoulders. "It's a good thing the kitty did get up there," she told him. "If we hadn't heard it crying we'd never have come to the stable today."

"Then 'tis a miracle—I'd have suffocated I reckon!" Mr. Crump sneezed, and sneezed again.

"Humpty Dumpty sat on a wall—Humpty Dumpty had a great fall!" began Beth.

"Shut up!" said Crispin briefly, for Mr. Crump suddenly leaned forward, resting his head in his hands.

Jenny saw that his lips were very blue. "Run, Crispin—tell Mr. Cameron," she said urgently, "and Beth—go and ask Mommy for that stuff she puts on cuts—and some tape, and don't take all day!"

Beth made a face, but she went, with Crispin at her heels. "Here's the walking stick—you'd better take it back," he said, picking it up from where they had dropped it by the stable door.

Beth took it, and caught the belt of his mackintosh as he turned to run down the lawn. "Why wouldn't you let me sing Humpty Dumpty?" she demanded.

"Because it's mean to tease someone when he's hurt," answered Crispin, "specially if he's old, or smaller than you!"

"Aren't you good!" taunted Beth, turning to run.

But this time it was Crispin who caught her. "Listen!" he said, "I'm not good, and I guess I never shall be. But I know God sent His Son to die for us a long time ago, and I'm going to try and show I'm grateful, and do what He wants. Aunt Anthea used to call it 'being a soldier and servant of Jesus Christ.' She used to talk to me about it, just now and then, when I was little—Sundays mostly—"

"How d'you know He wants you?" asked Beth sharply. "He might only want grown-up people—"

"Because Mr. Cameron says so." Crispin let go of her and gave her a push towards the hole. "Go on and get the stuff for Mr. Crump's cut," he said. "I've got to get down to the house. But I tell you this—" he added, "it's much easier to be mean and hurt people, and tell lies than it is to be a soldier and servant like Aunt Anthea said." He turned and sped down the lawn, leaving Beth staring after him, and for once she wasn't laughing.

Mr. Cameron was writing in the study when he

looked up and saw Crispin. By the look on the boy's face he guessed something was wrong. He pushed away his papers and hurried to meet him. A few minutes later they were up in the stable, and Beth arrived carrying the First Aid box, a small bottle of milk, and a saucer.

"For the kitten when we get him down," she said, giving them to Jenny.

Mr. Cameron looked concerned when he saw how shaken his old gardener seemed. "If you can walk now," he said, "I'll give you an arm down to the house. I expect Mrs. Mundell had better wash that cut before Jenny tapes it up for you. What made you climb on the hay, anyway?"

He looked up at the trap door towards which Crispin was already mounting. "It came on zo mizzling wet, Zir," explained Mr. Crump, as he got stiffly to his feet, "zo I thought I'd have a look up in that liddle old loft—haven't been up there fer donkey's years. Not since I worked fer old Mr. Cameron. Couldn't understand why he had all this hay, fer 'e never kept a horse to my knowledge. I just climbed up it easy, and shoved up the trap, and than I heard the cat somewheres. It jumped up on the hay and than into the loft—I stepped back on they bales—"

"And down it all came!" Mr. Cameron looked up at Crispin's legs, which were all they could see of him as he peered into the loft, coaxing the kitten. "Take care," said their old friend. "We don't want any more accidents."

He left them, giving old Mr. Crump the support of his arm as they went down towards the house, and Jenny followed.

"I want to get up the ladder!" said Beth and Jon both at once.

But Crispin called down, "Hang on a minute—I've got him, but he's scratching a little!"

Gingerly he backed down the wide rungs, clasping the kitten with one hand. Beth poured out the milk and set the saucer on a fallen bale. A moment later the little stripey creature was crouched over it, lapping feverishly, while Jon watched, fascinated.

"We'll shut the stable door so that he doesn't slip out again," said Beth. "I'm going to take him home and see if Mommy will let us keep him this time—he looks awfully thin. I want to see up in the loft first though!"

So Crispin helped Jon up, and Beth followed. Soon they were standing among a jumble of old chairs, crates, and broken pictures.

"There's another trunk here—what an awful lot of traveling somebody did!" Beth went across to lift the heavy rounded lid, while Crispin turned over a pile of dog-eared books. Jon made patterns in the dust on the window with one finger, and felt pleasurably creepy as he touched the festoon of spider webs around the frame.

For several minutes there was silence except for the gentle patter of rain on the roof, and then Beth's excited voice called the others to come and look.

"What is it?" asked Crispin, abandoning his pile of books.

"Clothes! Strange old ones! They smell of mothballs!" Beth reached into the deep trunk and pulled out a pair of buttoned boots, a parasol, and a silk shawl which slid through her fingers as though it were alive.

"Boy! They are old!" Crispin found a rusty-looking top hat, and Beth, reaching deeper dragged out a long curtain of dark green velvet. "It's beautiful!" she exclaimed, wrapping herself in it. "And look—here's a comb with glittery stuff on it—"

She set it in her golden hair. "Look, Jon! I'm a queen!" Jon was delving in the trunk like a terrier after a rabbit, and Crispin had just lifted from the bottom a metal box with a small padlock.

"Wonder what's in here?" he said, half to himself, and put it down behind him at the edge of the trap door, while he explored further.

"I've got a hat!" announced Jon, who had unearthed part of an Admiral's uniform. He put the cocked hat on, and giggled because it came down nearly to his shoulders, blinding him entirely.

"Here I come!" squeaked his muffled voice as he stepped forward waving an old scabbard with both hands. Beth was over by the window when she turned and saw him, and Crispin jerked his head out of the trunk as he heard her scream, "Jon! Jon—stay STILL!"

But Jon, suddenly afraid, swung around, just as Crispin flung himself forward. He caught the little boy right on the brink of the yawning hole behind them, and they fell together beside the opening. Beth, hampered by her cloak, managed to grab Crispin's belt before he could roll over and down through the hole.

Jon's kicking feet hit something hard which went spinning down from the loft.

There was a tremendous crash below, and then an awful silence as the three sat up with pounding hearts. Jon was too terrified even to cry.

"Something's broken," said Crispin at last. "I'd better go down and see what we've done."

Beth began to cry. "You saved Jon," she gulped, "I couldn't have reached him—he might have been killed!"

"Cheer up, he isn't dead anyway. You'd have stopped him yourself if you'd been nearer—" Crispin started down the ladder. As Beth got up and rather shakily began to push the old garments back where they came from, they heard him shout.

"We've smashed the little tin box I found in the trunk—the hinges have come apart, and the floor's all over foreign stamps—millions of them!"

9

Treasures for Everyone

Mr. Crump sat by the kitchen fire drinking hot tea, secretly enjoying being fussed over by Mrs. Mundell and Jenny. He had just been persuaded to take a second cup when the three children burst in upon them.

Crispin carried the tin box with its lid askew, and Beth clasped the purring kitten to her. "Where's Mr. Cameron?" asked Crispin urgently. "We couldn't see him in the library—"

Hearing his name as he passed through the hall, Mr. Cameron looked into the kitchen. "What's that you have!" he inquired, and Crispin handed him the box.

"I'm afraid we've broken it," he said anxiously. "We didn't mean to—we dropped it out of the loft!"

Mr. Cameron opened the box with a startled exclamation, and then tipped the contents out onto the kitchen table. Foreign stamps, of every size and color, mixed with hay and dust, spilled out over Mrs. Mundell's clean cloth.

Jenny pounced on them with a cry of joy. "These are tremendous! I collect stamps—I haven't seen any of these kinds before!"

She ran her fingers through the pile, and Mr. Cameron bent over them, his eyes lighting with excitement. Even Mr. Crump got stiffly from his chair to see the hoard.

"These be some of those what the old master wer always buyin and sellin," he growled. Mr. Cameron began to sweep them back into their box with a hand that shook a little.

"They are a wonderful find," he said. "I know a certain amount about stamps—enough to tell me that these old ones could be very valuable. It's a good thing you children started rummaging! I'd heard of course of my uncle's collection when I was young—the Curtis Cameron collection was well known. I had an idea he'd broken it up and sold the stamps long ago—"

"He used to have great big books with stamps arranged in them," remembered Mrs. Mundell. "But the last year or two before he died I never saw them. Perhaps he took them to the loft after we had that burglary."

Mr. Cameron sat down in the rocking chair, stretching his long legs on the hearthrug, where Jon sprawled stroking the kitten.

"Tell me," he said to Mr. Crump, "how long ago was it that he gave you notice and said he didn't want a gardener anymore?"

Mr. Crump scratched his ear and thought. "Seven year or more I reckon," he said. "It must have bin after I left that he got all that hay. Put it there to cover the ladder I guess, so no one would know what was hid up on top."

"He never had a horse to eat hay, did he?" asked Beth. "There must have been horses once though, but how did they ever get them into the lane?"

"Ah! well," said Mr. Crump, "there was gates you see, a long time ago. They was bricked up before my time. Just that liddle square hole left with a shutter—to put manure and such like in fer the garden, but the hay could be pitched over the wall I reckon."

"And we broke the shutter!" Crispin picked up a few stamps which had fluttered to the floor. He thought what a lot had happened since they had first looked through to the garden only three days ago.

Jenny had been sitting looking thoughtful. "Didn't you ever see this house when your uncle was alive?" she asked Mr. Cameron. "And why did he want you to live here when he died?"

"I saw it several times when I was a little boy," the old gentleman told her. Then he paused for so long, lost in thought, that it seemed as if there was no sound in the world except the ticking of the kitchen clock.

"My uncle had two brothers," he said at last. "One was my uncle Alfred, and one was my father. Old Uncle Curtis never got on very well with Father, so he hardly ever invited us to see him. We used to have holidays at hotels in Dover, and I loved the castle like Crispin does, but we were only invited to this house for very formal meals—I was never allowed to explore the garden."

"And the other brother?" prompted Jenny, who loved family histories.

"Uncle Alfred?" said Mr. Cameron. "Oh, he was the favorite! He came here often, and his sons did, too—my cousins. When my own older brother John grew up, he used to be invited, too, though I never knew why."

"Mr. John!" cried Mrs. Mundell eagerly. "I was

fond of Mr. John! He was always full of fun. When he married he used to come a lot, and later he brought his daughter here—your niece, Sir—Miss Christine—she was beautiful!"

For some reason that Jenny couldn't understand Mrs. Mundell looked long at Crispin as she said it. Mr. Cameron glanced across at him, too, but his face was sad. "Ah well," he said, "they're all dead and gone, and I'm the only one left. Though one day I trust I shall see them again in God's good time. That's why the house was left to me—" he added.

"Even your niece, Miss Christine, is she dead, too?" asked Beth, wide-eyed.

Once again there was a long pause before Mr. Cameron answered: "It is believed so. But it's a sad story, perhaps one day I may tell you, but not now—"

He got up stiffly, and helped Jon to his feet. "Away with you all!" he said, quite kindly. "This afternoon you may come and help me discover what else is in the loft. Bring Simon with you if he's not too busy. I shall probably catch the late train to London with these," he added. "If they are worth what I think they may be I won't have to consider selling this house, and the old roof could be properly repaired."

"Cheers!" shouted Jenny and Crispin. Jon added, "You won't go away! Yippee!"

"Reckon them's the 'treasure' old Master used to talk about" said Mr. Crump, grumbling under his breath as he accidentally kicked the kitten.

Mrs. Mundell swooped down and lifted it in her warm, capable hands, "Why—poor little thing, how thin it is! It's half starved!" she exclaimed, and hurried out to the pantry with Beth and Jon at her heels.

When Jenny looked in to call them to come home, they were kneeling on the floor, watching while the kitten ate, with rapturous speed, some fish which had been intended for Mr. Cameron's supper.

A little while later they all trooped up the path at Sunnyhill, calling for Mother.

"Oh shucks! You've got that kitten again!" said Simon, who was busy screwing up some extra shelves. He looked hot and bothered.

"I thought Mother said—" he began.

But the others shouted him down. "It's a stray! Mrs. Mundell says it is!"

"It's starving—"

"We'll look after it all ourselves!"

"Look after what?" asked Mother as she came downstairs. "Oh NO!" she began when she saw it, but four pairs of pleading eyes were too much for her. The kitten turned and gazed at her, with eyes that were too big for its little face.

"It showed us the way through the hole to Mr. Cameron," said Jon, "and we'll call it Stripey!"

"Anyway," added Beth, "if it hadn't got into the loft we wouldn't have found the foreign stamps—"

"Stamps?" Simon was immediately interested, and even Mother sat down to hold the kitten while Beth and Crispin told the story.

"But Jon—Jon might have been killed!" she cried in consternation.

"Crispin saved him," said Beth promptly, and Crispin flushed with pleasure.

"Beth's got two sides," he thought, "nice, and nasty.

Perhaps she'd be a lot nicer if she 'belonged,' like Mr. Cameron said."

That afternoon all the Bernard children went to help clean out the loft. The rain still dripped steadily from the great trees by the stable, but that didn't trouble the busy people inside.

Simon and Mr. Cameron, armed with screwdrivers, levered off the lids of some small wooden crates, while the others rummaged in a pile of junk. There were dusty old fire screens, wicker chairs that were falling apart, and several pairs of old high boots.

The clothes in the chest intrigued Mr. Cameron. "They must be from my grandmother's day," he said. "I believe she was a great hoarder, and wouldn't throw anything away that she thought might be of use."

The crates seemed to contain only heavy old books in leather bindings, but the last crate they opened made up for all the rest.

There were books in that one, too, but with a difference. They were stamp albums, carefully numbered.

As Mr. Cameron sat on an empty trunk and began to turn the pages of the biggest one, the children gathered around full of excitement. Most of the stamps they had never seen before, and the delicate old designs fascinated them. Even the names of many of the countries were different from the ones they had learned at school.

"That's because the map of the world is changing so fast," Mr. Cameron told them.

They were so absorbed that Jon startled them by announcing, "I've found another treasure!"

His 'treasure,' dragged out from under a roll of old carpet, proved to be a big Victorian needlework box, full of small trinkets, and dozens of buttons.

"Oh!" exclaimed Jenny. "What a lovely box! It's got mother-of-pearl all over the top!"

Mr. Cameron glanced at the contents. "You can have it if you like, Jenny," he said. "I can't imagine myself doing embroidery! You can have these oddments, too, if you like them—"

As Jenny thanked him with delight, he rummaged in the old box with his bony fingers and pulled out a small round case. "Here!" he said to Simon, "here's a compass—might be useful to you some day."

Simon took it eagerly. "I want to go sailing as soon as I can. I'd like to work on a sea-going craft—I guess I'll have to have a compass sometime—thank you, Sir!"

"I thought you wanted to be pilot of a Hovercraft," said Beth.

Crispin looked up quickly. "If you do, Simon, you can sign me on as crew!"

"I thought you only liked old things, like the castle—" said Simon, surprised.

But Crispin answered, "I like old and new together. After all, you've got a picture of the Golden Hind over your bed, and that's not exactly modern."

"You're too clever by half," said Simon, but his voice was friendly.

Mr. Cameron still rummaged in the needlework box, and found a tiny wooden boat for Jon, who was mystified because it wasn't made of plastic.

"That hadn't been invented when this was carved," Mr. Cameron told him. "How about this for you, Beth?"

He held up a little glass globe on a square white base.

Inside it Beth could see a tiny model of a church, with a house beside it, and a miniature person standing on a bridge. Suddenly Mr. Cameron shook it, and to her surprise the whole globe was full of whirling snowflakes.

"Oh, its gorgeous! Can I do it!" cried Beth, as the snowstorm began to settle, and one by one they shook it, and marveled at the tiny imprisoned scene.

It was Jenny who remembered that Crispin had nothing out of the treasure box.

Mr. Cameron was looking at a small, worn Prayer Book, which had spidery writing on the flyleaf. Jenny wondered if Crispin would want it, but Mr. Cameron slipped it in his own pocket.

"Belonged to my grandmother apparently," he said. "But the print is too tiny for me. Do any of you children go to church?"

"All of us," said Simon. "We go with Mother, and Dad if he's home."

"But there hasn't been a Sunday since we've been here," said Jenny, looking anxiously into the box, hoping Crispin wouldn't be left out.

But he was soon satisfied, for right at the bottom she found a small colored print in a thin frame.

"A knight in armor!" she said. "That's just right for Crispin!"

When Mr. Cameron handed it to him, Crispin said at once, "I've seen this picture before somewhere!"

Simon looked over his shoulder. "It's called 'The Vigil,'" he said. "Dad told me about it. Young men used to kneel and pray all night before they were made knights in olden times. They prayed for help to be brave and truthful, and clean in their minds—and that they might always help people who were weaker than themselves—"

"And then they had a cross put on their shields," said Crispin thoughtfully. He tucked the picture into his jacket, glad to have it for his own.

Simon turned to gather up the stamp albums, and hand them carefully to Mr. Cameron who had gone halfway down the ladder. "I've just noticed something," he said, "every one of these books has three 'C's stamped into the cover—they must have been made specially!"

"Charles Curtis Cameron," came the answer. "We all had a 'C' in our names. My grandfather was Christopher Curtis, and so am I. My father was Clive—there are three 'C's on all sorts of things in the house, I find."

Up in the loft Crispin stood as if paralyzed. Three 'C's—there had been three on the silver box on his chain, and now it was gone forever. Was it possible, he wondered, that he had some connection with this place where he felt so happy? Why had he let Beth tease him about the only thing he had ever possessed! The others scrambled down the ladder with their treasures, talking and laughing, but Crispin was a long time following.

10
Crispin Disappears

Crispin and the four Bernards helped carry all the precious books down to the house. They hung around watching and chattering while Mr. Cameron packed them carefully into a suitcase.

"Now, if Mrs. Mundell gives me a quick cup of tea," he said, "I'm going to get a taxi to the station. I hope that in a day or two I may have some exciting news for you."

"When will you come back?" Beth looked up from the library hearthrug, where she had found an ancient pair of bellows, and was teasing Jon by puffing them at him.

"Tomorrow possibly—or Saturday. It all depends. I don't stay in London longer than I need to nowadays."

Mr. Cameron snapped the suitcase closed. "I suggest you go and show those trophies to your mother," he said, giving Jenny a friendly pat on the shoulder, and they knew themselves dismissed.

They woke next day to find it still raining. The wind had risen, and was buffeting Sunnyhill with violent gusts.

"No good out of doors today—it's moldy and miserable," grumbled Beth, and even Simon was at loose ends.

Mother was glad that Jon at least was happy, playing with Stripey. Jenny was content, too, helping to make her own new dress, though she hated standing still while pins were stuck in everywhere.

The only excitement that morning was when a van from the furniture shop delivered a new bed for Crispin. "Now you'll be more comfortable than you were on that old camp bed," said Mrs. Bernard, as he bounced gleefully on the blue mattress.

But Beth was furious. "It isn't fair!" she cried. "If anyone has a new bed it ought to be me—I've only got Jenny's old one!"

"You know perfectly well," her mother told her, "that you've been whining for Jenny's bed for the last year because it's white with flowers on it. This one is simple and dignified. Just right for Crispin."

"Then Simon ought to have it," muttered Beth sulkily, "and Crispin ought to have Simon's—he likes old things—even the silly old chain around his neck—"

"I like my own bed, thank you," Simon told her curtly, "and anyway it's no business of yours. You're selfish, Beth."

Crispin bit his lip hard. He longed to tell Beth what he thought of her, too, and all his pleasure in the new, comfortable bed evaporated.

He stayed, rearranging his few books on the little shelf beside it after the others had gone. He leaned on the windowsill looking at the castle, but it was black and forbidding against the stormy sky.

"I guess I'd better tell God I want to belong to Him,

and ask Him to help me," he thought. But somehow he found it difficult to talk to God with Simon's transistor blaring on the landing below, and Jon being a jet plane up and down the hall. He chose a book to read and went downstairs.

Beth had found her 'snowstorm' and was dancing about with it, shaking the little glass globe to make a violent blizzard.

Crispin took his book and curled up on the low windowseat in the hall. He began to read, and soon forgot the others, absorbed in the excitement of exploring the South Pole.

Suddenly Jon's voice brought him back to reality. "Mommy! Mommy!" the little boy was shouting, "Stripey's going to be awfully sick on the kitchen mat!"

"Oh, no! Not my new mat!"

Crispin heard Mrs. Bernard pushing away her sewing table in the sittingroom and he jumped up. "I'll grab him!" he called, and dashed out to the kitchen.

He seized the heaving kitten and put it firmly outside the back door. He had forgotten Beth, but she was right behind him, still clasping her glass globe. Crispin banged the door and swung around, nearly knocking Beth over. She grabbed at the sink to save herself, but the snowstorm went spinning to the tiled fioor.

"Oh Beth! I didn't mean—" began Crispin, truly contrite.

But Beth turned on him, blazing with anger. "It was the best thing I ever had and you've smashed it!" she shouted. "Why did you ever come here? We didn't want you, and I hate you! Why don't you go away!"

"BETH!" Suddenly Jenny was there, red with shame

for Beth, and sorrow for Crispin. Sad, too, because the quaint old snowstorm was broken, and she knew that they would never have another.

"I've said I'm sorry," muttered Crispin, and he ran blindly up to the attic. Beth subsided in a passion of weeping, and nobody took much notice when a few minutes later the front door banged.

An hour later Mother found a very subdued Beth and Jon doing a jigsaw puzzle together on the kitchen floor, while a contented Stripey played nearby. "Where's Crispin?" she asked.

"He's gone out," said Jon. "I saw him. He's got his jacket on."

"Perhaps it's just as well," said Mother with a sigh. "He'll walk himself cheerful again, I hope." But by dinner time Crispin had not returned, and she began to look worried.

"He's probably in the stable," suggested Simon, and went to look. Jenny set the table, and Beth actually offered to help her. Beth had a cold, ashamed feeling inside, and was wondering what Daddy would have said if he'd heard what she shouted at Crispin.

Simon came in with the rain dripping off his hair. "He's not there, and he isn't at the house either—I went down and asked Mrs. Mundell."

"It's thoughtless of him, he must know the time—" Mother gave Simon his usual big helping, and added, "Of course he may be given to going off when he feels upset. After all we don't know him very well, but he doesn't seem that kind of boy to me."

The meal was finished and cleared away, and still there was no sign of the truant. "If he's not back soon we'll have to go searching," said Mrs. Bernard, though Jenny and Simon were certain that hunger would finally drive Crispin home. But as the afternoon went by and he still didn't show up, they began to look worried too.

"I wonder if he's down at the harbor?" Jenny went to the window and watched the apple tree swaying in the wind. "He said yesterday that he loved to watch a very high sea," she remembered. "I should think the waves are terrific down there now."

In the hall Simon was already struggling into his boots. "I'm going down, Mom," he said. "The silly kid might get himself washed away—"

"I'm coming, too!" said Jenny quickly. "I can go along the sea front one way, and you the other, and we can ask at the pier."

Mother helped her into her raincoat, and her kind gray eyes were troubled. Suddenly an enormous bang seemed to shake the house. As Jon and Beth came rushing into the hall there was a second loud bang.

"What was it?" quavered Jon, as Simon opened the front door and let in the wild wind.

"Maroons!" said Simon. "Dad told me maroons are a kind of fireworks. They fire them to call the lifeboat out."

Suddenly Beth threw herself into Mother's arms, sobbing. "It's my fault!" she gulped. "I was horrible—I told him we didn't want him, and now something awful will happen—"

When Simon and Jenny reached the harbor they found that they needed to stick together to make any headway in the gale. Tremendous seas were breaking over the promenade, and leaving small pebbles scattered all across it. Inside the distant harbor bar, ships of all kinds and sizes were sheltering.

"It must be worse out in the Channel!" Simon shouted as they headed into the wind, and began an exhausting search of every boathouse and shelter each time the waves receded.

There were few other people out, and none of them had seen Crispin. The Pier was closed, and there was no sign of him by the inner basin. At last, buffeted and cold, they turned for home.

"He's probably toasting his toes by the fire and being fed by now! I'll skin him if it's just been a prank—" growled Simon.

But no such good news waited for them. One glance at Beth's tear-stained face gave Jenny a sick feeling of dread.

"Come and have something hot!" Mother took one look at Jenny's white face, and felt her icy hands. "No more going out tonight for you," she decided. "But Simon may have to go and phone the police. Aunt Anthea left Crispin in our care—I wish Daddy were home. He'd know what to do."

"Mr. Cameron would!" said Jenny quickly. "He may be home—he said it might be today—"

"I hope he is!" Simon was out of the door before Mother had time to think. Five minutes later he startled Mrs. Mundell by thundering on her kitchen door.

When Crispin left the house that morning he had come to a decision.

In spite of the wind and rain, he was going to try something which he had been planning ever since

Simon mentioned the three 'C's on the stamp albums.

Somehow he was going to get back his silver chain and the battered little box attached to it. Then he was going to write to Aunt Anthea and ask her to take him away.

Although he had gone out of the front door of Sunnyhill, no one had noticed him go around past the kitchen window and down the garden path to the shed. He knew a coil of thin rope and some tools belonging to Mr. Bernard were there, as well as a tall iron spike with a round 'eye' at the top. Jon had found it under some rubbish, and Crispin guessed it had once been used to tether a goat.

In the dimness of the shed he hunted for the rope and a big hammer. Then he wrapped them, with the spike, in a piece of sacking. Quietly he slipped out of the garden door. He had enough money to pay for the bus, and half an hour later he was trudging up towards the castle gate in the driving rain.

Nobody was out on that wild September day. He kept well away from the tower and the restaurant, where a few visitors might have gathered. There was something else Crispin intended to do, even before he tried to retrieve his chain. Because of that he followed the path which led under the great trees and sharply uphill, towards the Pharos tower.

Today the trees were rather frightening, with the wind making them roar like the sea below, but Crispin went on. Up there, where the old Romans had built so well, he was going to make his prayer to God.

At last he stood inside the protecting walls of the sturdy old tower and leaned against the ancient stonework, his breath coming short and fast after the steep climb. He felt alone in the world, and yet he was glad to be there.

He guessed that long ago William the Conqueror must have stood just where he was standing, and the tower had been ancient even then.

It was very old indeed, Crispin thought, when the first Queen Elizabeth had come there with her glittering nobles and great ladies. But all down the centuries ordinary people must have come to the tower and to the old church behind it. People who wanted to be alone, and to ask God to guide them in their lives and help them to be brave.

"I can't make a vigil like the knight in the picture," he thought. "I haven't got enough time. But I guess God will understand if I keep remembering that Jesus died on the cross so that all the things we do wrong can be forgiven. I guess He'll understand that it's too difficult to be good all by myself, however much I want to be like the knights who carried the cross on their shields."

Then, with his head bowed on his hands, he asked that he might be a true soldier of Christ, who alone could help him to fight those things which were wrong in his life, as well as all other troubles which might come.

"And now I'm going to be happy," he said to himself, "because I know I belong. Best of all, I know I'll never be alone any more!"

He went outside again. The wind caught him and sent him racing down the path, thinking as he went, "I'm not going to hate Beth, whatever she says!"

Five minutes later he was beside Peverell's Tower, and running along the wall to find the arrow slit. Would the chain still be there, he wondered fearfully, as he pressed his face against the damp stonework, and looked down. Then his heart gave a bound of joy, for he caught the glint of silver as the little trinket swung in the wind. The crow's sharp eyes had missed his treasure.

His next problem was how to reach it. Nearer the tower the wall was lower, and he could scramble up and rest on it, gripping with his elbows.

He could see the arrow slit quite well from there, and that was all he needed to guide him. He slithered to the ground again and undid his clumsy parcel, glad that he had taken the time to knot the rope all along its length before he left the old shed.

The squally rain beat on him violently as he took the hammer and drove the iron spike into the wet earth beside the wall. He hammered and hammered till it was well in and firm. Then, with hands that shook a little from excitement, he slipped the end of the rope through the 'eye' and knotted it.

Now he was ready, and, throwing the whole coil over the stonework, he scrambled up to watch it go snaking down towards the moat. To his relief it touched the grass, and with infinite caution he wriggled around till his legs were on the outside of the wall.

Heights had never bothered Crispin. He had always done well at climbing in the gym, so now, as he gripped the rope firmly and let himself down, his heart beat fast, but not with fear. It swung uncomfortably, knocking his knees and knuckles against the rough stones, but at last his feet touched the grass. A few minutes later he was scrambling along, slipping and sliding, till he came below the arrow slit.

How terribly far up above him it looked, but nothing was going to stop him now. For just above him his silver chain dangled in the wind.

Joyfully he grabbed it, and slipped it over his head. The box felt cold as it slid down against his skin.

"I'm hungry now!" he said aloud, and realized for the first time that he was going to be shockingly late for dinner. But even so, he felt lighthearted as he caught the swinging rope and began slowly, and painfully, to work his way up.

Many, many times he had gone up a rope to the roof of a gymnasium, but this was far higher, and the wind tore at him as though it would drag him away.

And then it happened. A great gust sent him spinning against the wall, and at that moment the old rope parted high above his head. He fell like a stone, down, down, down.

How long he lay unconscious in the long grass at the bottom of the moat Crispin never knew. When at last he drifted up into the world of sight and sound again, he had forgotten where he was.

He stared upwards into a dark sky, and the great rushing sound of wind seemed to fill the whole world about him. When he turned his head a blinding pain made him cry out, and then he saw above him shining walls that seemed to reach up into heaven.

It was not for many moments that he realized the wet cold earth beneath him must be the bottom of the moat. Then he knew that the shining towers were the castle walls made more beautiful by the floodlights. That meant he had been missing from Sunnyhill for many hours.

"They'll never find me here!" he thought with panic, and then, as he tried to move, the pain engulfed him again. As always, when in trouble, his hand groped for the silver box. At the same moment he remembered that he belonged to Someone who would never forsake him.

"Please, God, help them to find me," he whispered, and slipped back again into unconsciousness.

It was nearly an hour later when sudden pain brought him back to reality. There were people around him, and lights. Someone, whose voice he knew, was saying, "It's a miracle we've found him—he feels half frozen—"

A big, warm, hand closed over his, and a blanket was tucked over him. And then another voice, which was surely Mr. Cameron's, cried out, "Look! See what he's holding! My old snuffbox—he's Christopher, not Crispin—thank God he's found at last!"

Then, in a daze of suffering, he felt himself lifted, and a strange swaying journey began which puzzled him considerably.

Lights hurt his eyes when he tried to open them, but he found the voices around him comforting. Surely it was Mr. Cameron who was sitting close to him when someone said, "We'll take good care of him—it seems he's very precious to you, Sir—"

"The most precious person in all the world to me!" came the heartfelt answer.

11
The Secret of the Box

It was many hours before Crispin knew what those words meant. He was wrapped in a comfortable sleep most of the time, but people came and went around him, and said kind things.

At last he was really awake, and knew that he was in that brand-new bed in the attic, and that Jenny and Mr. Cameron were sitting beside him.

"Hullo! I believe he's going to take some notice of us at last!" Mr. Cameron sounded relieved, and told Jenny to run and fetch her mother.

Crispin wanted desperately to say something, but he found it difficult at first. "Will she—will she be cross? I was awfully late for dinner—"

And then Mrs. Bernard was there, kissing him, and crying a little, and saying that the dinner he missed was yesterday's.

Jon and Beth crept in, very quiet and shy, but their mother shooed them out again. Turning to Mr. Cameron she said something which puzzled Crispin very much. "I'll leave you to tell this boy of yours all your news. The doctor said he'd be fit for it when he woke.

I'm going to heat some chicken broth and we'll see if he's hungry."

"I'm STARVING!" cried Crispin, suddenly finding his voice, and trying to sit up at the same time. But his head still ached dully, and he leaned back and listened while Mr. Cameron talked.

Briefly he told Crispin how Simon and Jenny had set out to search the harbor. Then, just as he had arrived back from London, they had come down to the big house asking for his help.

"But how did you guess where I was?" asked Crispin wonderingly.

"I think it was a God-sent inspiration—I knew your love for the castle, and I understood that Beth had been rather unkind. It occurred to me that you might have gone up there if you were miserable, but it was quite dark before Simon and I arrived, and began to make inquiries. No one had seen you, but a search was started at once, and then we came across the stake and hammer by the wall. The short end of rope hanging over told us where you were, and then the men of the cliff rescue service came to help us. But my boy," he added, his voice still kindly, but a little stern, "I can't imagine why you should do such a hare-brained thing—why did you want to get into the moat?"

Crispin's hand went to his neck and found the familiar chain. "For this—" he answered, a quick flush sweeping up to his forehead. "I—I threw it away the day you took us up there—I thought perhaps it was babyish to wear a locket thing. Then I wanted it again; you see it has three 'C's!"

Mr. Cameron leaned forward, his kind old eyes alight

with joy. "I know it has," he said, "because it was mine years ago. And it was your great-grandfather's before that—Christopher Curtis Cameron!"

And while Crispin stared at him, wide-eyed, and scarcely daring to believe that the wonderful news was true, Mr. Cameron told him who he was.

"You'll remember, Mrs. Mundell mentioned a 'Miss Christine,'" he said. "Well, she was my niece. And my dear boy, she was your mother, and she called you Christopher."

"My mother? But how can you tell?" whispered Crispin.

"She and her husband were great travelers," his great-uncle told him. "Your father was a wonderful photographer, and he worked for a travel magazine. Even though you were tiny, they took you with them. I was traveling a good deal myself at the time, and I met them in Athens one spring.

"It was the first time I had seen you, young fella, so I thought you should have a present!"

Crispin lifted the silver box, a question in his eyes. "Yes—that's it!" said Mr. Cameron. "I hadn't anything suitable to give a baby, but I took the old snuffbox from my pocket—I used to keep postage stamps in it in those days. We put a few peas in it to make it rattle, and you laughed at it. So your father punched a hole in the corner, and your mother supplied the silver chain, and we hung it on your crib."

"And then?" asked Crispin, holding the box very tightly.

"Then I said good-by, and I never saw them after that," his great-uncle told him sadly. "They left their car to be repaired in Athens, and said they were going on a tour of the Greek islands. But they were never heard of again.

"There were some terrible earthquakes that spring. People were buried in landslides, and drowned in floods. I believe they may have changed their minds and gone inland—it seems so, from the place where I understand you were found—Mrs. Bernard has told me the details."

Crispin drew a deep breath, and lay back on his pillows. "So I DO belong!" he said at last. "I belong to you, don't I?"

"You certainly do, and how glad I am to have you! D'you think you will like to live in Dover for good?"

He need not have asked, for Crispin would have leaped out of bed with delight if he hadn't been far too stiff, and if the chicken broth had not arrived at that moment.

"Aunt Anthea will have a big surprise," said Mrs. Bernard smiling. "But I'm sure she'll be as happy for you as we are."

Mr. Cameron sat watching as Crispin ate hungrily. "You had a pretty terrifying experience, my boy," he said after a while.

"I ought to have been awfully scared," answered Crispin truthfully, "but somehow I wasn't, because I knew I belonged to God—" He pushed away the tray, and without shyness told how he had made his own 'vigil' at the Pharos. "And I'm going to wear a cross on my shield now," he said as he ended, "you know, Uncle, the shield that's always there although you can't see it—O.H.M.S.!"

"That's the best decision you've ever made, or ever will," came the answer.

And so, very content, Crispin slept again, to be wakened, hours later, by a small weight pressing on his chest. A loud purring in his ear told him that Stripey had come to pay a visit, and a moment later Beth came looking for him.

She was still somewhat subdued as she sat down on the bed, and began to stroke Stripey's silky back.

"I want to say I'm sorry," she said bluntly. "They didn't tell me to, I came by myself."

"I didn't go up there because of what you said," answered Crispin, "I was going anyway."

Beth nodded, "I know," she said. "Simon told me about the box on the chain, but it was me that made you throw it away, and you might have been killed. So I've made a vow—"

"What sort of vow?" asked Crispin, interested.

"That I'll count ten before I say horrible things," said Beth, shamefaced. "I'm going to remember that bit about my tongue being like a fire—I'm not going to let it burn anymore,"

Crispin's blue eyes met hers in a friendly grin. "You know some fires warm people," he said, "they're comfortable. I guess when you say kind things like your mother and Jenny do, you light that kind of fire."

Suddenly Beth smiled back. "I s'pose you do—I never thought of that!" And then she added eagerly, "Did Mr. Cameron tell you? About the foreign stamps, I mean? He's selling them to a big dealer in London, and he's going to have a new roof! You can choose any bedroom in the big house for your very own—and

Mr. Crump's going to make a proper door in the wall by the stable, so we can all go in and out."

"Goodo!" cried Crispin, suddenly finding he could sit up without hurting at all. "So you can have this new bed if you want it," he added, giving the mattress an extra bounce.

And then he wanted to get up, because the television was on downstairs, the good smell of toast told him it was time to eat, and Jon was being a Hovercraft up and down the hall.

"Go and tell them I'm starving again!" he commanded Beth, and slid out of bed. He took a few stiff steps toward the window, and looked out. It was a still evening, with fog rising. From the harbor came the plaintive sound of a tug hooting, and above the mist the castle rose pale and mysterious.

Crispin felt so full of happiness that he wanted to shout and sing. Now he belonged for always to the old town down below, where the lights were beginning to twinkle. Now he had a real uncle to claim his love and loyalty. Now the castle would always remind him that he belonged to that great company who, through the ages, have been soldiers of the Cross.